W9-AEP-882

BULLIES

BULL

STORIES

Little, Brown and Company—Boston—Toronto

IES

George W. S. Trow

FIRST EDITION

All the material in this book
originally appeared in *The New Yorker.*

LIBRARY OF CONGRESS CATALOGING IN PUBLICATION DATA

Trow, George Swift.
Bullies.

I. Title.
PZ4.T8595Bu [PS3570.R645] 813'.54 79-28278
ISBN 0-316-85305-4

BP

Designed by Susan Windheim
Published simultaneously in Canada
by Little, Brown & Company (Canada) Limited

PRINTED IN THE UNITED STATES OF AMERICA

for Veronica Geng

• ONE •

I Expand My Horizons

One of the things I've done since last year, when I got my divorce, is to expand my horizons. I have gone through a period of rapid personal growth. This has had nothing to do with exterior circumstances. As before, I live at the Keowa Motel and take my meals in my room. The growth I'm talking about is creative growth, interior growth, the kind that counts.

I have learned to focus my energy. You may not be familiar with the Arica Training. I am. In the Arica Training one learns the concept of "chich." "Chich" is *noise* — the interior distractions that keep us from focusing our energy. I strive now to reduce the "chich" in my life. One way I do this is by staying in bed. On many days I choose to stay in bed for the whole day. What I do is I stay in bed and concentrate on one thing. I focus my energy. On one recent day I stayed in bed and focused my energy on "humidity." This resulted in my resolving a long-standing conflict. I feel completely in touch now with the "humidity" of my living space, which is important to me because the Keowa Motel is incredibly damp all the time, with one thousand little molds growing everywhere and small drops of moisture condensing on the cinder-block walls — *out of nowhere* condensing, merging, running down the walls to the damp floor, and so on.

I have done more than just learn to focus my energy. It would be false modesty not to mention that I have founded a major dance company — The Jack Duff Dance Experience (I am Jack Duff). The Jack Duff Dance Experience is devoted to Movement. The Jack Duff Dance Experience seeks to transcend the limits of Dance, as Dance has been defined by conventional, institutionalized dance groups. Let me try to make this more immediate. Right now. Right now I am lifting my left leg. There. My left leg is *off the ground.* Now my left leg returns (slowly) to a position *close to its original position* but not coincident with it. This has been what The Jack Duff Dance Experience calls a VM, or Valid Movement. Even in the Keowa Motel (where The Jack Duff Dance Experience is currently headquartered) it is possible to complete hundreds of VMs in the course of a single afternoon. Very often I spend my day in Valid Movement. Sometimes, by contrast, I spend my day observing the little molds that grow in the damp corners of my rehearsal space. Either way, I call the shots around here.

There is a rehearsal this afternoon. My friend Bob is coming over. I have made Bob a full partner in The Jack Duff Dance Experience — not in the sense of stock and so forth, which I retain, but in the sense that I invite him to rehearsals. He has been slow to understand the implications of his own movements, I'm afraid, but I will be patient. He has a very nice shuffle step (the result of an injury sustained on an icy stoop), which nicely complements my own lack of balance. So far, I have had to trick Bob into developing his talent for Valid Movement. Sometimes, feigning weariness, I ask him to get the beer from the icebox. (My suite at the Keowa is a housekeeping unit, as you will have guessed.) Under the impression that he is doing me a favor, he shuffles over to the icebox and shuffles back with the Genesee. Entirely valid, and justified, as all great movement must be, by *purpose*. At the end of rehearsal, Bob and I fall asleep in our chairs.

As part of my ongoing personal growth, I am making plans for the future. I am planning, for instance, to build up a new and more meaningful wardrobe, from scratch. In making my plans I have been very much influenced by the New York *Times Magazine* and by an expensive soft-cover book entitled *Laid-Back Luxe*. My cousin Charles (who went to Wesleyan) had his picture in the *Times Magazine* not long ago. He was photographed wearing an embroidered coat from Afghanistan while picking out a head of Bibb lettuce at a downtown vegetable market. The caption under this picture explained that my cousin Charles was an "amateur gourmet." My cousin Charles wrote a little bit of text, and this appeared next to the captioned picture. It would be difficult to reproduce Charles' style in paraphrase, so I will reproduce it word for word. He wrote:

> Weekdays I feel very Brown Shoe, very coat-and-tie. I still have a Glenurquhart plaid suit I bought at The Andover Shop at New Haven, and I wear it once a week, religiously. But weekends are different. I call them my "Me Days." I wear a mix of whatever — old flannels, the crazy coat I got in Kabul (I liked myself in Kabul), and I do what's right for *me*.

I have great respect for my cousin Charles. I especially like the way he has managed to imply that he went to Yale. For a number of years now, my cousin Charles has done all his errands in New Haven. He drives from New York to New Haven to do all his errands. He gets his bridgework done in New Haven, for instance, and then when the subject of teeth comes up he says, "Do you know, I still go to my old dentist in New Haven — isn't that silly?" This technique, over the years, has been strangely effective. I feel that Cousin Charles is now beginning to imply that he went to Andover.

Although my cousin Charles has been a big influence on me since my divorce, although he has made me see the importance of setting aside certain periods of time *just for me* and my own *personal style,* he has not had quite the effect of Maria Atris, the author of *Laid-Back Luxe.* Maria's favorite person is a man named Riccardo Tuscani, who does exactly as he pleases. She writes:

Riccardo is a space salesman for an important advertising agency, and also a film critic of great wit and distinction. Ask Riccardo to drinks one day and he'll arrive *à la Valentino* in gaucho garb; see him for lunch the next day and he'll be dressed head to toe in leather, like a male hustler. Riccardo likes to break things (vases, glasses, desk sets — anything that seems obnoxiously self-important and fragile), and he will often appear with shards and fragments of broken objects stuck raffishly in his lapel.

Thanks to my divorce and one or two other failures, I am learning to express myself in my dress. More and more I am coming out of my shell. I am learning that clothes can relate to Valid Movement, and I am planning to design an entire Valid Wardrobe to express my own feelings about the interaction of body, body covering, and body environment. I am thinking about ways in which body coverings can facilitate and enhance the processes of tripping and falling down, for instance.

Sometimes, though, in spite of my new focused energy and my new dance company and my new plans for my new wardrobe, I find myself experiencing slight problems of adjustment. Sometimes I find myself resenting the molds in my rehearsal space. Sometimes I find myself eager to throw my ex-wife down a flight of stairs. And sometimes I find myself wishing something terrible would happen to my children. Terrible, I said — not fatal. And not an accident. Nothing where my ex-wife could nurse them round the clock and buy them fuzzy bears to cheer them up. I have in mind something more subtle, like — a drug problem. I think if my children had a drug problem I would have to go to be with them myself, even if it meant postponing or cancelling the inaugural season of The Jack Duff Dance Experience. If I sacrificed my inaugural season my children would be touched, I think, and would give up their drug problem in gratitude.

But these problems of adjustment are minor. They are no match for my new inner strength. Already I am making plans for the *second* season of The Jack Duff Dance Experience. I have planned several series-of-related-movements.

One of the important series-of-related-movements planned for the second season will deal, in a nonprogrammatic way, with my rug at the Keowa Motel. What interests me is the way my rug strives to express its identity (and its growing awareness of its strength as a rug) in modes that challenge traditional norms. My rug, when you get right down to it, really refuses to function as a floor covering. Like my ex-wife, my rug wants to exist in a nonjudgmental atmosphere. "I am not here to meet your expectations" — that's what my rug says to me. I have learned from my rug. Just now, on the way into my rehearsal space from my icebox space while executing a complicated Valid Movement, I chanced to drop my beer glass. My beer glass landed on one of those patches of floor that my rug now declines to protect. My beer glass shattered, and instead of giving in to the old tiresome drop-spill-mop-up guilt, I think I will take the fragments of broken beer glass and stick them raffishly into my T-shirt and then lie down on the floor and learn to relate to the spillage.

Alani Beach Now

RIGHT NOW, THE VACATION VALUE IS BACK WHERE IT USED TO BE. AT ALANI BEACH. Right now. Right here. The little fish that were dead are swimming again; the big hotels that had to close for a while (because of all the talk) are open. Many times, the sun shines — on the sidewalks, on the park benches (many of which have been repaired), on the beach itself.

ALANI BEACH AND THE WHOLE ALANI AREA ARE MORE NEARLY ALIVE THAN THEY'VE BEEN FOR YEARS. The drugstores have new, expanded security precautions. Restaurants that had to close because of the small green snails appearing suddenly everywhere have opened for certain things. The patches of damp that had invaded the concrete — crumbling the walls, infesting the hidden supports, heaving up the foundations until buildings collapsed without warning, until hundreds, maybe more, were trapped, buried alive, condemned to a death-in-life, choking for breath in the rubble, gasping out cries of help, but no help, none, all gone — these patches of damp have been identified, plastered over, repainted, and swathed in absorbent material to aid in the temporary relief of excess moisture.

THE WATER IS BEING REVITALIZED. Many curious and advanced processes, relying on the most expensive technology, have been utilized in Alani Beach's effort to reinvigorate the water. Special agents hostile to the red stinging plants that have recently been afloat, clinging together in red clumps like coagulated blood, multiplying on the richness of the sludge, easing through the disposal drains into the pools, into the pipes, choking off every simple flow of liquid, turning the water into a kind of grotesque jelly — special agents have been put to use to encourage the helpful instead of the hurtful side of this disastrous act or vengeance of God.

ALANI BEACH IS YOUNGER THAN EVER BEFORE. The oldsters have packed up and left. It's a different story now. No more depressing oldsters clogging the sidewalks, sitting in those railed areas — talking, talking, talking. No more oldsters walking up and down. We shut off support services, drove up the cost of food. We were tough, because we knew we were fighting for the future of Alani Beach. Now, instead of oldsters we've got discos, and shops selling jade and Oriental objects and electronic calculators at enormous markdowns.

THE UNUSUAL BARS ARE OPEN! On the rubble of the area where we had to go beyond cosmetics and actually demolish a number of badly compromised buildings, there is now an amusement zone. You can tell by the little spring in people's step, by the way they look quickly, then away, that it's an amusement zone. People come in quiet, leaving the hotels with perfect security, under cover, not open to the night, taken safely in huge transports painted green. Not the failed green, from the military, from the holding pens, from the epidemic spread, no, not that green, based on wasting chemicals, flaking off into the hand at the lightest touch, no, not that green, but another green, more soothing, more resistant to rust, *another green* is used to give color to the transports, to the fun. In the amusement zone, people go their own way, in quiet. Some people adopt special themes: medical themes, themes with special clothing. In certain unusual bars, people have permission to wear the new leggings, the new serious leggings, leggings that can be worn tight against the damp, against the cold, leggings that give a thrill of constriction as they are laced tighter and tighter, changing the texture of the skin.

AND THE RESUSCITATED HOTEL REINE-AMERICAN IS AT THE CENTER OF IT ALL. Walk in the door: there's new green matting everywhere. The international cartel that has assumed ownership of the fabled Reine-American has invested in coco matting and hundreds of thousands of swaths of special absorbent material to help prevent leakage. Special underground swimming pools, hundreds of meters beneath the surface, guarantee a glorious dip in pure water in secure surroundings. Special "shufflers" — unique shoes resistant to fungal growth and to the powerful fungicides in use to combat fungal growth — are available at poolside. Alarm devices, designed to alert guests on a *room-by-room basis* of a successful invasion of the concrete by the killing damp, have been installed and can be activated by feeding in fifty-cent pieces. Complimentary decks of playing cards have been placed in many rooms (and all suites) for use during the terror.

Glut of Stars

THIS WEEK, next week, and in the weeks that will follow the next week, and for all the time after that, there will be a glut of stars at the Hotel Reine-American. Sitting at the bar, stirring those old drinks we used to love — the ones made with cream, with bitters, with colored syrup more potent than any whiskey: our stars. Waving across the lobby — our enormous lobby — wearing jaunty scarves tied around their necks: our stars. We have our stars in our entertainments and in our benefit theatricals. On our staircase — our famous staircase, winding down from the ballrooms — our stars pause to wave. From any kind of distance, the figures of the stars seem like sad little sticks — standing on our staircase, standing in our enormous lobby, waving their hands like sad little sticks. But up close they are the same as ever. The stars we used to love, from the old times when we loved the stars. When we loved them to play up like ladies and gentlemen in *Avenue Parade*, and *Swing Fall*, and *The Roentgen Story*. When we loved Saly Begley singing his great songs in *Guam Canteen*, and *But Not for Them*, and *Morning*. They're back. In tiny suites, efficiency apartments. At the Hotel

Reine-American. They went away for a while, but now they're back. In the Hoyden Room. In the Bush Lounge. In the Catalypse Ballroom. At the Hotel Reine-American.

In those old days, we had nothing but stars. We knew about them. We knew the way Dorothy Yoir wanted her hair parted — all that hair, the way it tumbled down, making her look so tall, so knowing, when she was just a half-pint and so innocent, so innocent, robbed by her agent, that man who had the oil scheme, who put her in films for his own profit, films like *Dark Road,* which were made with no skill, which showed her small size and, then, her age. We knew about her. We knew how old she was, and how much she owed.

The stars went away for a while, but they are back. The stars take extra care now — that is the only difference. They walk in shorter steps — that is the only difference. Sometimes they stay in their rooms. Sometimes they walk up and down in the wide, airy corridors. Sometimes they will not move. Sometimes they stay totally still, as though they were waiting for something to happen — that is the only difference.

Now, and for some time to come, Saly Begley sings in the Catalypse Ballroom. Saly is moving slowly now — that is the only difference. His throat is tied up with odd pieces of cloth to keep out the damp — that is the only difference. He wears a caftan — that is the only difference. He carries his chin high, for reasons we know. He takes extra time in preparing his numbers, because he only wants to please. There was a time when he carried a small knife in a place just under his arm. There was a time when he was taken through the crowds by Tom Jussy and Frankie Vers, who knew how to squeeze and press a limb until it was dead. There was a time when he took the tower, the whole tower — not one room left for anybody else. But now he only wants to please. He takes extra time to please, to get the phrasing right on "Velvet Night and You," and "My Sad Hand," and "Poor Boy Ride." He says, "Thank you, ladies and gentlemen, thank you, thank you."

Sometimes when Saly says "Thank you, ladies and gentlemen, thank you, thank you," our supervisory hostess laughs at him, just in fun. And then she insults him, just in fun, and then some of the other stars get up and hit him — ineffectual weak blows but with enough force to throw him off balance. At times like this, people remember Myna Rous, that enormous woman of seventy or eighty or more than that, who went so far back into the beginnings of the business that it was impossible to know if she antedated the beginnings of the business. People remember her special brand of earthy humor and her whispered intonation and the way she pushed people off the stage when she wanted to, using her knee and her short, stubby fingers, laughing and laughing while people fell, laughing while they slunk off, laughing while they pretended they liked it, pretended not to hate her for her temper and her fat and her incredible age. A few years ago, we named a special corner of the

Catalypse Ballroom for Myna Rous when she tripped and fell headlong down the stairs of the entrance of another hotel, which had failed to install the special friction pads necessary during the damp.

Stars keep coming back and back and back to the "Renny," and the "Renny" keeps on making new friends among the young stars — the stars from the newer times just after the times when we loved the stars, from the times when we began to have a different attitude, when the stars began to be more like us, not like the girl next door (who would be Molly Gest, the last Megam ingénue, who lives at the "Renny," thin now, and gaunt, her cheeks collapsed into her mouth in a way that precludes public appearance), not like anyone next door, but more like us. The young stars were shy at first, because they remembered the "Renny" legend from the days of their growing up, when Myna Rous and Lou Wedge and Frankie Spuri entertained for government figures, when the "Renny" was headquarters for the Claims Damage Settlement Commission, when Myna Rous whispered a shocking song that only she could get away with, shaking the giant hips that were hers alone, and caused a general laugh among men who did not laugh. They remembered when "At the Renny" meant beach spats on the beach, draperies trimmed with expensive fur, and diesel-powered buggies, attended by Southern people, running from the elevators to each room. They remembered a spirit of elegance and formality, and of course that spirit lives on: in the intensified security precautions (courtesy lines in the lobby, identification formations in the function areas, employees who know each guest by smell and touch), in the special measures against the damp, in the expensive friction spikes that are everywhere — everywhere walking is allowed — to scrape off the film that tends to accumulate now on the feet. But there is also a new spirit at the Reine-American, a spirit offered up in the spirit of the new stars, and influenced by them, by their way of life, by the way they toss the jam spoons onto the floor with a laugh, by the way they wrap their skin in shreds of old clothing bought *anywhere* — at shops run by people who scavenge in the old buildings, at thrift shops for the poor people, people with every kind of trouble.

The new stars have different needs. We know that. The new stars need special hot lines, special provisions for crisis intervention. The new stars want edges that can hurt. On certain days, their food must be served as kind of a gruel. We know it. But we find that the new stars also like many of the conveniences traditional at the Reine-American. The new stars like room service, for instance. Sometimes we don't let them have it, just for a joke. Then they have to queue up. Some stars are waiting for the elevator right now. People come up close. People breathe on their skin to test its tone and texture. People pass along smiles of recognition and go back to their own places in line.

Moon Over Alani Beach

It was unexpected, the way the moon appeared suddenly, after so long an absence, as though there had never been any clouds at all, as though the dust from the peeling hotels had not mingled with the gas steaming up through the land, had not risen to the low evening sky and hung there for months and months and months, producing a morose mood and physical danger and a distorted sense of time that was a feeling of perpetual twilight. In that twilight it had been impossible to judge distances, for example, or trace light to any simple source. Everywhere in the sky there had been a stagnant phosphorescence, like a visible echo of artificial light. Then the moon came out, and the teasing glow vanished in a minute, only lingering for a while in the pockets of bad land, the recent land built too far out into the harbor, too far into the marsh, where the gas continued to rise, would always continue to rise.

In the moonlight, it was possible to see from one end of the causeway to the other. People looked up. The moonlight showed the great hotels along the beach, their height intact, rising twenty or thirty stories, running together (as it appeared from the causeway) like a crazy wall built to different heights and in different styles at different moments, like a wall with a purpose, a fortification. People moved at a faster pace after seeing the familiar buildings and did not mind so much just where they stepped.

At the end of the causeway, at the place where the old highway had debouched into the Avenida de las Palmas, the principal boulevard of the Spanish Colony, a great fat man, dressed in pleated pants that conformed with perfect accuracy to the eccentric bulge of his enormous stomach, walked around the rotting barricades, kept his shoes clear of the mud, kept step to a puffing rhythm he made with his breath. He did not look at the moon but looked, rather, at the shadows thrown by the old hotels across the Avenida de las Palmas. His eyes moved from left to right, attending to the geometry of the shadows, while he kept up the puffing noise with his breath. He proceeded to the middle of the old Avenue, where there were two strips of land on which remained certain hardy grasses and certain palms that had not rotted in the damp and, between the two strips, a third, on which there was nothing. He walked in this third strip, seemed at home in this strip. He kept on at a steady pace that was different from the pace of the few other people on the Avenue — less furtive, more like something confident running on tracks than a man afraid of the night. At the intersection of the Avenida de las Palmas and the Avenida de los Alpes he made an easy curving turn left toward the waterfront, toward the shadow of a hotel. Before entering the shadow, which was the shadow of the Hotel Merovingian, the greatest of the luxurious hotels of the colony, having been built to incorporate every luxury with every satisfaction of historical memory, having suffered a contraction and damage from the damp but still throwing a fine shadow, the large man stopped his puffing noise. Then he looked up quickly at the moon and went into the hotel.

When the moon came out, Madame Ludovica saw it strike the mural in her room at the Merovingian and she looked at her watch, which was a man's watch, a big watch with a sensible leather strap, because Madame Ludovica was sensible about time, and mail, and the way a writing table is arranged, and the way bills are paid or not paid, and the way exercise is taken or not taken, and because she was not vain. The time the moon appeared, Madame Ludovica was prepared to say with certainty, was 10:06 P.M. At one moment, she was looking at her mural and there was no moon. At the next (she did not shift her eyes meanwhile, or blink), a powerful silver light came into the room and imposed the pattern of the window onto the mural. Madame Ludovica took this as a sign. She stayed exactly where she was and watched. She was tempted to go to the window to see the effect of the moonlight on the city, but she did not.

She looked at her mural, kept her eyes on the mural. She watched the pattern made by the moonlight pass across the mural. Madame Ludovica felt something rise inside her. She knew what it was: a form of concentration very like hysteria. Madame Ludovica had slit her wrists once when she had allowed herself to concentrate too deeply. She had felt herself to be a river and had wanted to flow in her own blood. It had been embarrassing, of course, but it had been pleasing, too, to feel the power of self-transformation at work. Since then she had made it a point to control the rising of the concentration, but she had not abandoned it or lost pride in its power. She tried not to talk to herself, or to strangers, because that brought the concentration on in an overwhelming way, and she tried not to touch things that appealed to her in her path, or to establish any special rhythm of walking. But she did permit herself to stare at her mural, all aspects of which she felt to be benign.

In the moonlight she stared at a figure in her mural — a man in early middle age, blond, with long hair and an expression on his face in which violence and beatitude were mixed. He faced forward into the room — toward Madame Ludovica, toward the window, toward the moonlight. The moonlight blanched his face and brought out (so it seemed to Madame Ludovica) the gentle understanding in his nature, for which the air of violence was merely a disguise. His right hand was extended in a gesture of welcome, and seven men on his right knelt in several positions along Madame Ludovica's wall to receive his grace. Madame Ludovica could not see the figures she knew were kneeling on his left, nor could she see his left hand or the portion of his face to the left of his left eye: all of this was in a room belonging to another guest of the hotel, on the other side of a thin partition. But this did not diminish her pleasure by much. At some moments, she regarded the truncation of her mural as a reminder of everything she had been denied, but for the most part she held to the conviction that the power of the mural in its entirety might be threatening. It was enough, she felt, that the central figure remained, almost complete, on her side of the wall. There was no inscription to identify the scene depicted in the mural, but Madame Ludovica was almost certain that the central figure was the barbarian Alaric and that the mural as a whole comprised a Visigothic court scene, for her room was a fragment (not a very large fragment) of the Alaric Suite, formerly the première suite of rooms at the hotel. Little historical evidence concerning the Visigothic monarchy had been made available to the artist, and he had included a number of decorative elements from other, better documented, courts, so that there was about this assemblage of Gothic nobility a distinctly Elizabethan feel, but this did not spoil Madame Ludovica's pleasure in it. In any case, her pleasure had very little to do with questions of accuracy. Her pleasure had to do with faith and with an interest in preserving the blond young man (the presumed Visigothic king) from the indifference he would be sure to face in any company but hers. Madame Ludovica, who was, as she put it, the last of the Hohenstaufen, superior in dignity to the Habsburgs, knew what indifference was.

Elsewhere in the Merovingian, the effect of the moon was subtle. Roberto Diaz-O'Malley, the proprietor of the hotel, was asleep in his rooms, a bottle next to his bed, a bottle bearing the label of an old brandy but holding a small amount of liquor of another sort. Roberto dreamed, as always, of kidnapping, which had been a vogue during his youth. In his dream a simple unmarked car, trained in evasive maneuvers, moved at various speeds along obscure routes, to no avail. As always, the route ceased to be obscure and became ominous. The undistinguished motif of the car became, in its anonymity, an announcement of the intent to evade, a declaration of privilege and foreign association. People along the route came out to look as the car went by. People noted that the speed of the car became erratic, as if the car were driven by a lunatic or a person in senility. They noted that the route taken was a route taken by no sincere person. They noted that the car was driven by a young man. Suddenly, then, a well-marked vehicle moving at a constant speed, no impediment acknowledged in its pace — a bakery truck, perhaps, or a vehicle for the transportation of children to a private school, a simple vehicle with all the time in the world — drew up close, and the kidnapping was effected.

At this moment in his dream, as always, Roberto

Diaz-O'Malley awoke with a sense of relief, of anxiety gone. He looked around his room, which was in disorder. He saw the damp in the stucco and the heaps of small dust accumulating by the sill of the door and under the windows. He saw his open luggage — old luggage, expensive luggage, luggage one person could not move without help — and his belongings in his luggage. He could not remember whether the luggage was being packed or unpacked. He saw the bottle at his bedside and put it to his lips. "How perfectly vile," he said. It was not obvious, even to himself, if he referred to the liquor in the bottle. He looked around the room again and was surprised to see how definite were the outlines of the disorder in the light through the blinds. The surprise, however, was only a flicker of interest across the workings of his obsessions, and he did not get up from his bed, draw the blinds, or see the moon. Instead he turned over so that he faced the wall, faced away from the disorder. "So like Managua toward the end," he murmured.

Cornelia and Consuelo La Salle, the famous twin sisters, now nearly eighty, took the opportunity of the moonlight to resume work on their dual autobiography. Cornelia held a snapshot up to the moonlight. There were two figures in the picture. One was a woman of startling beauty, her eyes held straight ahead in an expression of final disdain, her mouth pursed into a tiny bow that managed to look inhuman without looking unfeminine, her neck — indeed, the entire upper half of her body — hung out with an enormous rope of pearls. The other figure had been scratched out with ruthless efficiency.

"Who is this, dear?" Cornelia asked, pointing to the rash of scratches on the photograph. "Who is this with you?"

"Just nobody, darling. I can't think why you trouble with that. I can't think where you *found* that."

"I think I recognize the *shoes*."

"I can't think why you bother, I can't think where you find these old scraps that haven't a bit of general interest, unless you've been creeping and pawing where you don't belong." Consuelo made a sudden movement at the photograph.

Cornelia hit her sister a rather strong blow across the shoulders and said firmly, "But lamb-pie, you know we must strive for candor. The public demands it. You know that they do."

Then Consuelo began to cry, and Cornelia, who was used to that, took the photograph to the window to have a better look.

In his tower room, Mr. Peter Stuyvesant, who had been having a sinking spell, first felt the presence of the moon as a rising of spirits. Frail, thin, and so old that he seemed beyond age, he had been lying on his wicker chaise longue without energy enough to prepare his broadcast. He had noticed several new raw spots on his hands and had wrapped them in a piece of fabric in such a way that little direct action was possible. He felt the power of the moon as an impulse to unwrap his hands. When he did, he found that the irritation had somewhat lessened. The spots were red, to be sure, but the white pustules of infection had withdrawn. Heartened, he looked about him and saw the moonlight. He rose at once, as though startled by the unlooked-for arrival of a beautiful woman. He went to his window. He could see across the causeway to the Beach City. He could see each of the big hotels. His hands rose from his side to frame his head in a gesture of pleasure. They trembled slightly, like the last leaves on a tree in the cold.

"My dear," Mr. Stuyvesant said, as he looked without blinking at the line of hotels, "there they are. Just like that."

After a moment he began to count the hotels, moving his eyes from right to left, and he looked exactly as though he were counting eggs under a hen. Then, when he had finished, he counted them again, calling them by name: "The Seurel, there is the Seurel, just like day, just like any day you please, and the Herez-Chenonceaux — the dear old Chenny — just like our lovely times in Tunisia before Tunisia went. There are the gardens! The gardens at the Chenny. Imagine that! And then the Yormin. Not my style. A little businesslike, the Yormin, but never mind. Then the Mogul-Delhi — too big for these times, the Mogul-Delhi, all those *wings*, but God bless it anyway, yes, God bless the Mogul-Delhi. And then the Reine-American, *naturellement*. How well the Reine-American looks. Quite like a queen. I must remember to say that. Then the others just as ever. The Tidal Riviera just as ever, the Gotham Sand just as ever, the Hollywood Plage just as ever. Then the causeway. How fine the causeway looks in the moonlight! And there are lights in the restaurant district. Oh, well! This is quite a relief, I must say that it is."

Then Mr. Stuyvesant moved away from his window and toward his closet. He took off the linen smock he wore when he worked in his archives and clipping books and put on a handsome smoking jacket with ingenious embroidered fastenings across the chest.

"Well, well, just like that," Mr. Stuyvesant said. "I really do feel that I should go on *live* tonight. I really do feel that I should."

The moonlight shone over the Spanish Colony and the Beach City and the mainland city. The moonlight showed changes in texture, but only when you looked closely. The moonlight seeped into the cracks, showed the cracks, showed the tiny fissures expanding from small bubbles of air (natural to the process by which dust is compressed into a wall that will bear weight), but only if you looked closely. From any distance, the moonlight showed beauty and an interesting geometry. In the moonlight even the badly compromised hotels — the Hollywood Plage, for instance, which was not a hotel at all anymore, really, where there was no security, none at all, come and go just as you please, every door off its hinge, every pipe clogged with the small red plants that bloom in wet decay, the underground arcade a nest of thugs and poor people, with every kind of trouble— even the lost hotels seemed to resemble their old selves if you did not look closely. And the buildings from the first boom, the old buildings in the Spanish Colony and on the mainland, these buildings seemed to expand and breathe, to take comfort in their abundant motifs. Most beautiful was the Palacio de Bellas Artes, which floated over the Cottage District on the mainland like a beached liner. A folly of the Aspair family, the Palacio represented every wrong choice: the choice for a Spanish motif when the vogue had passed for a Spanish motif; the choice for enormous aspiration, for a doubling of size and an immensity of decoration when it had become quite clear that people were more and more reluctant to enter under a roof in any large numbers; the choice for fine art imported from European circuits—European opera that no one cared to hear, European dancers whom no one wanted to see; the choice for a location in the northeastern zone of the mainland city, which had been laid out for mansions, which was to be a neighborhood of unexampled luxury, but which failed to catch on, which failed even before the general failure, which had not even the distinction of triggering the general failure, and which, although it continued to carry the official name Districto del Mar Azul, had come to be called the Cottage District, after the maze of small buildings that began to spread out in every direction. An utter failure before any failure was common, the Palacio de Bellas Artes was suffered to remain because its failure was so complete that tearing it down would pay no one. But in the moonlight, suddenly, it gave comfort.

Madame Ludovica, on the causeway, looked up at the beach hotels, but just for a second; she looked back at the Spanish Colony, but just for a second. For the most part, she kept her eyes on her feet. A boy, an unpleasant boy, walked behind her, and she wanted to give an air of quiet determination; she wanted to close her mind so that he would have no place to enter. The boy was alone, but he was the sort of boy who belonged to a pack of boys. Madame Ludovica knew how it was. At first, there was just one, challenging you to be rude, ready to be hurt, his eyes full of accusation and a sense of injustice; then, when the insult was established, out of nowhere would come others to redress the wrong — boys who could not be persuaded, usually, to stop at robbery. The trick was not to see the first one, to shut him out of your mind, to keep your mind far from the possibility of insult, far from the revulsion you would feel if the situation were acknowledged. Revulsion was the insult the boys provoked most often, and the one they punished with most cruelty — that, and fear.

Madame Ludovica made it safely across the causeway and went to the Hotel Yormin to meet a friend. No one had better security than the Yormin. She felt the attention of the stray boys turn away as soon as it was clear that she was going to the Yormin. Entrance to the Yormin was through a series of narrowing doors — not doors merely, but sensitive detectors, which detected metal in suspect configurations, and plastic, and the new admixtures of metal and plastic that people found under their chairs, or along the molding, or under the edge of the table, and that were more powerful than other small explosives. The last doorway was not only narrow but designed to mold itself close to the figure. Guests of the hotel and a very few important people had a card key, which, when placed under a scanner, kept the doorway from effecting this final intrusion; but Madame Ludovica did not have such a key, so she was obliged to stand patiently while elements of the doorway shot out toward her body.

Once inside, Madame Ludovica was attended by a member of the concierge service, a red-faced boy who seemed to be losing his hair in patches: bald welts the size of silver dollars showed all over his scalp. He took Madame Ludovica up in the elevator.

"I wonder if you know my friend Mrs. Grendle?" the boy asked suddenly, with a quick sideways jerk of his neck.

Madame Ludovica said that she did not.

"It's Mrs. John James Grendle. Mrs. Montgomery Grendle, she calls herself now. She had an awful divorce." This information the boy imparted as though it added particularly to the woman's importance.

Madame Ludovica smiled, but did not answer.

"You'd be surprised how *she* treats me," the boy said ominously.

Madame Ludovica said nothing, and the car arrived at her floor. The doors opened six inches above the level of the hall. The boy made no effort to bring the elevator down. Madame Ludovica stepped down carefully.

The boy looked at her morosely. "Just like a friend. That's how *she* treats me," he said.

Madame Ludovica looked at him, putting revulsion and fear at a distance. "That's very attractive," she said, smiling.

Her friend kept her waiting — waiting at first when he did not immediately come to the door, waiting afterward when he stuck his head out and told her to wait. Then he let her in, and Madame Ludovica saw that he had company, a tall man dressed in a black suit that was much too big for him. Madame Ludovica wished that she had telephoned ahead, but she had not thought to do it, because she had little money; because the only telephone that worked at the Merovingian was the public telephone in the lobby and she was afraid to stay too long in the lobby; because she had thought only of the moonlight. She did not know of which she was more ashamed — her poverty, her fear, or her enthusiasm. Madame Ludovica was in most circumstances a sober and sensible woman, but when she felt herself to be in the wrong, she adopted a manner that was much too lighthearted. Her talk was too lighthearted now. She said several lighthearted things and watched them compress the faces of her friend and his visitor. So unhappy did this make her that she was about to leave, when the man in the dark suit rose himself.

"Things were going smoothly," the man said, as though Madame Ludovica had been the cause of a change of fortune away from the smooth. He pursed his lips and pulled his face into a deep, deep frown. "Things were going very smoothly."

It seemed then that the man in the dark suit would not go, that he had got up for some other purpose. It seemed to Madame Ludovica that it was expected that *she* would go, but she did not know how to leave, since she had only just come in after a long wait in the hall. She was embarrassed by the rudeness of her friend, and this led her to adopt a manner more lighthearted still. Her hands fluttered in a gesture of surprise, and she ran to the window in a girlish way.

"Oh, oh! Look at that moon!" she said, pulling apart the curtains, exclaiming at the moon but not looking at the moon — looking, instead, at the dull concrete buffer area below, seeing herself shattered on the pavement, lying perfectly still and unembarrassed, lying there, perhaps, for days, because people did not go much into the buffer area even when there was a job to do. The job of picking up a shattered woman would not be one the hotel would rush to complete, Madame Ludovica thought.

"Please close the drapes," Madame Ludovica's friend said. Madame Ludovica turned around and saw that the man in the dark suit had left. Her friend did not rise or offer her a seat or offer her refreshment. "What can I do for you?" he said.

After a very brief conversation Madame Ludovica left her friend and was out in the hall again. She dreaded ringing for the elevator and thought about taking the stairs, but she was on a high floor and staircases were unprotected, even at the Yormin. She rang for the elevator, and after a while it came up empty, unattended by any member of the concierge staff. Reaching the lobby, she directed her eyes to her feet to avoid any chance of seeing the red-faced boy, and she left quickly. Outside, the air seemed a bit heavier than before. She had intended to eat in a restaurant as a treat, but she headed for the causeway instead.

Madame Ludovica thought, I can get to the causeway. There is no problem about getting to the causeway. I will not look to the left or to the right. Then Madame Ludovica looked to the left; there was a laugh and a scream of pain, and Madame Ludovica looked to the left. She could not see a thing. Nothing. Whoever had screamed was not there; whoever had laughed was not there. Madame Ludovica moved on. She felt the air growing heavier. She passed by the Reine-American. Her ankles began to hurt badly, and she wanted to wrap them up. She had two pieces of red cloth in her purse. She wanted to take them out and put them around her ankles tight. She looked up. Ahead of her was the Tidal Riviera, a hotel where things were in doubt, where sometimes there was someone to protect you and sometimes you had to pay extra not to be hurt. Beyond the Tidal Riviera was the Gotham Sand, and then the Hollywood Plage, and then the causeway. Madame Ludovica felt a hand on her shoulder. She turned to the hand. There was a tall fat man dressed in a huge black suit, a small black tie, a white shirt with a tiny collar, like a joke on a collar. The moonlight brought out the paleness of his skin, and another quality — the smoothness. The pores had contracted to produce an unnatural smoothness, like baby skin over scars.

"Feeling a little tired?" the man asked.

"Oh, no," Madame Ludovica replied. The hand of the man did not leave her shoulder.

"You wouldn't like to lie down?" the man asked. He gave a smile, like a joke on a smile. Then there was a threadbare scream, the remnant of a scream, the sound of a slap, and then Madame Ludovica looked to her right, toward the sounds. She saw another man, like the man who stood with her, and a woman, not standing but sprawled on the ground. The woman looked up for a moment and held Madame Ludovica's eyes, shaking her head back and forth. Madame Ludovica turned to the man standing with her.

"No. No," she said. "I feel quite recovered, thank

you. But I do want to thank you for your time." She reached for her purse, and she felt the hand of the man withdraw from her shoulder. She gave the man the money she had planned to spend for her dinner treat. In taking her money from the purse, she exposed the red cloth she used to bind her ankles, and she blushed for shame and fear; but the man said nothing, and she went on her way, quickly, afraid to look to her left or her right, afraid to see the woman sprawled on the ground.

The air was growing heavy, and clouds crept up from the periphery of the sky. Madame Ludovica walked as quickly as she could. She did not look at the Tidal Riviera, which was deeply compromised, where the management was deeply compromised, where you had to hire private security, because the management would not, where the best of the private security people now declined to go; she did not look at the Gotham Sand, which was a place sustained by gamblers, by people who gambled on the progress of the silt creeping into the disposal drains, on the rate at which the cottages built on the bad land sank and decomposed, on any danger; she did not look at the Hollywood Plage, which was the worst; she did not slow her pace or look up until she reached the causeway.

At the causeway the red-faced boy was waiting for her. She pretended not to recognize him, lowered her eyes, and walked at a pace in which she had put her trust. The boy followed her. She felt his footsteps. Then he began to mutter. She could not understand him at first. Then, insensibly, she slowed her pace to hear.

"I know her business," the boy said. "I know her business, I guess."

Madame Ludovica might have altered her pace to be out of range of his repetition, but she did not.

"I know her business," the boy said. "I guess I know it well enough."

The phrases were sounded over and over, until Madame Ludovica began to repeat them herself. "I know her business," she said silently. "I know her business, I guess."

The air grew very heavy. From the middle of the causeway it was not possible to see anything but the causeway. The Beach City and the Spanish Colony were dead to sight. Madame Ludovica and the red-faced boy walked in step. Then, after a time, the boy fell quiet, and a little while after that, he turned on a radio. All the time he kept in step with Madame Ludovica, and she kept in step with him.

Mr. Stuyvesant went on the air at midnight. He wore his smoking jacket, and he was assisted by Jaime Diaz-O'Malley, the young son of the proprietor of the Merovingian. He went on live, but he used material from his archives, because it was his opinion that contemporary material lacked allure. He sat straight up next to the microphone. As he went on the air, he smiled and took a deep breath.

"This is Peter Stuyvesant reporting to you from the frontiers of fashion, where chic never sleeps," he said.

Consuelo and Cornelia La Salle heard him. "Why, I think Mr. Stuyvesant's gone on *live,*" Consuelo said. "I'm sure that he has."

"I'm sure *he'll* recognize this photograph," Cornelia said. "That man has a mind like a steel trap."

"Oh, I don't think it could mean a thing to him," Consuelo said.

"I think he'll recognize the shoes," Cornelia said.

"I don't think it could mean a thing to anyone who didn't take a nasty interest in every silly thing," Consuelo said, and then she began to cry.

Madame Ludovica heard the Peter Stuyvesant broadcast on the causeway. "He's gone on live," she said. She turned to face the boy behind her. "He's on live tonight," she said, "because of the moon. Because we have the moon."

Madame Ludovica and the boy walked on together, listening to the broadcast. Mr. Stuyvesant mentioned so many of her favorite items that Madame Ludovica felt quite recovered. He mentioned the party at the Merovingian when Bernard Fram gave to each guest a colored glass goblet, each more extraordinary than the next, each the work of a year, and then demanded that they be thrown onto the floor and shattered. He mentioned the sale at Las Olas, the great Aspair property that had stretched across the tip of the mainland, a fraction of which property had yielded speculative land enough to make five fortunes. He mentioned the vogue for the word "*blasé*" pronounced as though it were "blaze" and then pronounced it that way several times. He mentioned the awful feud between the La Salle sisters and hinted at a cause — an interest shifting from one sister to the other on the part of a member of the House of Windsor. He mentioned the painful divorce of the Adolpho Stewarts, and he mentioned the vogue for a Brazilian actress. Then he said, "Madame Ludovica, the last of the Hohenstaufen, is the most exclusive royalty in the Spanish Colony. When she takes tea at the Marsh Club, Madame Ludovica, who eschews all titles, breaks a piece of toast under the table and spreads the crumbs in a circle to symbolize protection from usurpers."

Madame Ludovica turned to the red-faced boy. "That's who I am," she said simply. "I am Madame Ludovica, last of the Hohenstaufen."

The boy looked at her quietly and said nothing. They walked on. After a time the boy stopped. "This is where I live," he said.

Madame Ludovica looked over the edge of the causeway. Sometimes on the slopes of the causeway there were clumps of cottages. For long stretches there was nothing — just land eroded down to the rocks upon which the causeway was built. But there were places where the land still sloped gradually to the water, and in these places there were a few cottages left — dangerous, but attractive in their motifs. There were cottages like thatched huts, cottages like the ones in the best illustrated children's books, cottages with trellises, cottages with Moorish arches, cottages in every popular style. On the slope near to where Madame Ludovica and the boy were standing, there was not a group of cottages but only one, on a bit of badly eroded land. It was done in a Spanish style. There was a big window — the glass mostly shattered but partly protected by an iron grate that was intact and had been recently painted.

"I love the Spanish style, don't you?" Madame Ludovica said to the boy.

"You treated me just like a friend," the boy said.

Madame Ludovica returned without incident to the Merovingian. Her spirits were very high, and she thought again and again of the days when she had taken tea at the Marsh Club, escorted to the same table inside the glass-covered court always by Jules himself, because Jules knew who she was — knew exactly who she was. Still, she felt a chill as she entered the Merovingian. The clouds had reached the moon and very nearly covered it. As she started across the enormous lobby — not secure now, not protected — she felt some sadness and some fear. She put these out of mind. She saw the tiles on the floor and thought how beautiful they were — handmade, each one, glazed with that dull glow that only certain workmen can produce. She stopped and looked at the tiles. She remembered throwing her goblet onto them. She remembered how the fragments of fine glass had looked against the tiles — the shards of colored glass each a fragment of perfection, perfect because shattered, perfect both in intent and in no intent. "Bernard was right to make us do it," she said out loud.

She walked on. The moonlight was fading from the room. There was barely enough light to see. She made her way to the staircase, and then she looked around. She looked at the great mural, the principal work in the hotel — an enormous representation of the Merovingian court on the occasion of the crowning of Clovis. The mural was punctuated by the phrase "White Faggots" and by the auxiliary phrase "White Faggots Die," and by renderings in cartoon of five large black phalluses, placed to impale the chief noblemen of the Merovingian Court.

Madame Ludovica turned away and stumbled. She felt something unexpected and soft. It was Bernard Fram, smiling and fat, sitting on the stairs waiting for the moonlight to pass, his pleated pants pulled up to keep their crease. Of all the guests at the Merovingian, only Bernard Fram went back as far into the past as she: only he and she remembered when the Marsh Club met in the Frankish Dining Room before it had a house of its own; only she and he remembered the private dock for yachts; only he and she remembered the Carolingian, the Merovingian's twin hotel, connected to the Merovingian by a marble subway. Yet they were not friends.

"Ah," said Bernard Fram with a smile. "Madame Ludovica, the proverbial bad penny."

Cornelia La Salle was at the window as the moon slipped behind the clouds. The photograph of her sister was still in her hand. "I think I know who this is with you, dear," she said to Consuelo. "Isn't it that *unnatural* little girl in Positano? The one who *just wouldn't leave you alone?*"

Consuelo's lips quivered. "I don't see how you could say she was unnatural. She was descended from all the doges," she said, and then she began to cry.

Cornelia turned away from the window and threw the photograph onto the floor, where there were many photographs and clippings and invitations, and even a number of visiting cards from the first and most respectable period of the sisters' youth. "Well, dear," Cornelia said, taking her sister's head in both her hands, and wiping away the tears with a certain tenderness, "you know what *they* were."

• TWO •

Friend Twin

It's Friend Twin. Looks like a friend, feels like a friend, gives off a little sigh of pleasure when you do things together. Friend Twin asks about your screenplay, supports you while you lie in the giant redwood steaming appliance and enter altered states (face down in the steam, all senses distorted, your arms, your legs all gone); Friend Twin does not steal your screenplay while you lie in the redwood steaming appliance, does not talk to an agent behind your back, does not take your press contact to La Grinn, the new Chinese restaurant where the banquettes are lacquered and the food comes in lacquered crates just like the special crates you can lock yourself into for darkness-accommodation therapy, only small.

Friend Twin is so much like a real friend that once he's seated at table, most people can't tell the difference. Friend Twin raises his arm. Friend Twin brings his spoon to his soup. Friend Twin talks about the deal Freddy Friyn has made with Barbara Krearn, which cuts out Marty Rupp and everyone else who had to leave the studio because they took the old silver sconces from the walls — those solid-silver sconces Lewis Routh had put in in the great old days, when he wanted the studio to look just like a private home. We knew Marty was unscrewing the sconces, slipping them away, cutting them into tiny pieces and taking them out in his hands. Sometimes the edges were jagged and his hands were cut. That's how we caught Marty — by matching the blood on the bare places where the sconces had been with the blood type on his hand, in his hand, in the veins of his hand. Marty has a special blood type, and he brought that up in a play for sympathy. Also the fact that he's been under a lot of stress. Friend Twin is sympathetic. Friend Twin understands about stress. Also, he knows all the gossip.

That's the thing to remember about Friend Twin. Maintenance is way down — he stays under the floorboards, up in the cramped bedrooms, anywhere, without complaint — but even so, he knows all the gossip. With a real friend, you'd have to teach him all the gossip and then you'd have to deal with his legitimate human needs. You'd have to listen to a lot of swinish talk about What I want blah blah blah, you never think about me fulfilling my needs blah blah blah, I want time to fire my beautiful blue pots in my kiln blah blah. Friend Twin has no needs. Friend Twin has no legitimate human aspirations. Friend Twin only wants to please. And he wants you to know the latest gossip — about the remake of *Woman Luck* with an all-woman cast, with Sally Undorn as the bitch and Fraan Harvey as the girl who has the wasting disease and Polly Morfer as the little one who has a lapse. He wants you to know. And he wants to help. Friend Twin only wants to help.

Friend Twin wants to know about any sexual quirks. Friend Twin is not judgmental. Friend Twin will stay quiet and watch. Or say what is appropriate. Friend Twin wants to help clean up. No matter what the accumulation. No matter how it looks. Friend Twin makes a note of it. But what do you care about that? It's natural that Friend Twin should make a note, keep it in mind, store it for later. Friend Twin only wants to preserve the link without imposing.

Remember when you left for a weekend? Spent the weekend in the black crate, deprived every sense of its function, lay there for days, waiting for the arms to disappear, for the legs to disappear, to feel that absence? Remember how your *old* friend — who came from where? the upper peninsula of Michigan, was it? — remember how your old friend stole into your apartment while you were gone and took your screenplay behind your back to the Ursa Company, the new company formed by the people who had the backing of people who couldn't come to town, exactly, who had to stay at a distance, but who had money, so much money? Can you see your old friend walking in the door? Friend Twin wouldn't do that. Instead, Friend Twin would help plan a dinner dance. Just for you, in your honor. Friend Twin has style. Friend Twin has class. Friend Twin knows the attractive caftans from the ones so ugly they eat into the skin. Friend Twin has so much style that sometimes he seems almost British. Oh, not the old British — Duke Marquis Earl — not that. The other British — all the same skill with artifacts, all that tight edge, but loathing the Dukes and the Marquises, and the Earls, hating the way the light hits the water, but willing to help out with pleasure. Friend Twin knows what you want. Friend Twin knows what you *have* wanted, don't forget that. Don't underestimate Friend Twin. Friend Twin will stand perfectly still, holding your caftan, but Friend Twin has his options, with all he knows.

Bobby Bison's Big Memory Offer

REMEMBER NOSTALGIA? Remember when you remembered the 1950s? Remember when you remembered the '60s? Well, it's all back. The good times when you remembered the good times. The laughter when you remembered the laughter. The *heartache* when you remembered the heartache. A treasury of everything you remember remembering. Remember remembering your first kiss? Remember remembering your first prom? Remember remembering your first name? Well, it's all here. Including your Mom, your Dad, and your dog Tige (if that was his name), just as you remember remembering them.

Who could forget remembering Suez? Who could forget remembering "circle" skirts? And where were *you* in 1972, when the world thrilled to the memory of price supports for butter? Yes, those were the '70s — *innocent* days when you copped a few "ludes" and remembered the Drifters, Larry Ferlinghetti, India's surprise attack on plucky little Goa. *Simpler* days, when all you had to do for a good time was sit back and remember malt shops, double dips, ponytails. Think back: Were you one of the lucky ones who remembered cruising the hamburger stand? Can you remember remembering the Jive Bombers, Herbert Brownell, juvenile delinquency? If you're normal, or close to normal, you cherish the memory of remembering these memories and regard fondly the gift of cerebral "recollection" that made it all possible.

Yes, you remembered it all in the '70s, the Golden Age of Nostalgia. And now, for the first time — the only time, the last time before it's all exported — Bobby Bison, the King of Nostalgia, is making available selections from *your own personal memory!* These are memories that are bound to be the most treasured memories you remember remembering — and many of them have never before been offered in this particular way! All the memories involved are the original memories of the actual memorable events themselves. *Not* a congeries of inferior, so-called "subconscious" memories, this is a definitive collection involving the actual process of conscious recall! Memories like this:

> I remember when my sister Margie got a new light-blue angora sweater — you know, the kind of sweater that was real fuzzy and you could wear it tight if you were built right, which Margie wasn't. Anyway, what I really remember is how Margie started to light a Cavalier cigarette and turned our whole house into a flaming inferno by dropping her match onto the angora sweater instead of in the ash receiver. I remember that because after the fire we both had to go to live with my aunt, who is someone I will always despise.

Do you remember remembering that? Of course you do.

Now, don't *you* want to recapture the way you remembered all your memories? Well, before Bobby Bison ships them off to oil-rich Iran, why not try to relive it all one more time? Don't delay, because Bobby is loading all your cherished memories on supertankers right now, and once they've gone around the Cape it'll be tough cheese on you. Of course your memories *want* to stay right here where you first remembered them, but you can hardly expect them to hang around if you forget to send in for them!

And now here's your own grandmother to tell you how to order.

Bobby Bison's Energy Budget for the Eighties

THESE DAYS if you press Bobby too closely about his energy budget, Bobby will get too anxious. Bobby has been under a lot of pressure. We have had to line his office with long strips of absorbent cotton — like the cotton found at the tops of vitamin jars but dyed black — to keep out the noise and light. Bobby has not had time for a haircut or a manicure, and he is a little depressed about his appearance. His fingernails, which really are much too long at this point, go *click-click-click* on the keys of his typewriter when he sits down at his typewriter to type up his Energy Budget for the Eighties. Sometimes just that sound (*click-click-click*) is enough to distress Bobby and he has to go back into semi-seclusion. We have suggested that Bobby *dictate* his Energy Budget for the Eighties to one of us, but Bobby doesn't trust us completely for a job of this sensitivity.

The Entertainment Group has suffered most. Geoffrey Nalendo, manager of several of our rock bands, has tried to get Bobby's O.K. for a spring tour for three of the new violent bands Bobby was able to sign when his fingernails were short; but Bobby just defers and defers and defers, and the final disposition — whether to go to Australia, New Zealand, across the industrial tier, or just to the New Jersey death-rock clubs — has yet to be made, and the bands are very restless, especially the Dead Geese, who could be very hot if they got the exposure, plus a real effort made for air play, plus product in the *stores*. Geoffrey Nalendo has had to keep a lot of the musicians under permanent sedation in order to prevent them from getting violently angry over the delay in promoting their careers. So, you see, from our end it is completely a holding action until Bobby finishes his Energy Budget for the Eighties. The idea that Bobby is *purposely* delaying the release of his energy budget is really not sensible, given the terrible strain that Bobby's whole organization is going through.

I'll run down some of the things that have come up so far to delay the energy budget. I won't go into every single detail, but I will give all the broad strokes. First of all, Bobby has felt a little *fat* lately — rolls of excess and so forth surrounding nearly everything he's done. Bobby thinks that he should be having a *trim* experience while he works on his energy budget. This has presented very real problems, because Bobby is able to eat only certain foods, many of which are high in bulk but very low in nutrients. Also, exercise has been difficult, because Bobby doesn't completely trust us and refuses to be strapped into the special exerciser we had made for him. Once, just for a joke, we *did* keep him in his special exerciser a little longer than was really comfortable for him, and I guess that preys on his mind.

There have been other things, which I will just quickly run through. Rich men being abducted in Italy: the statistics worried Bobby, and to get him back to work we had to export certain of his friends from Italy to keep those abduction statistics from going right over the top. Then the day-to-day affairs of the Sulfurlands Sportscomplex took up a lot of his time: stock raids on the Kronos soccer team, special considerations for the award-winning forwards (their personal lives — divorce from unsuitable starlets and so forth), all of which had to be handled by Bobby personally, because only he really has the clout. Then there was the question of a possible buy-out by Multi-Promo (Bobby's holding company) of all outside-held Kronos stock in the Sulfurlands umbrella organization (which had to be approved by both governors, because of Sulfurlands' bistate mandate); and then there was the dissolution of the Great Gamble Underwater Safari Park (because of revocation of its casino license) and the resale of its assets to the 54 Fifth Avenue Corporation, which is Bobby's real-estate trust. All of this took a lot of time. Meanwhile, Doris Bison, Bobby's wife, whom Bobby resettled in the Canadian west in the late nineteen-fifties, began to make a *lot* of noise — speaking to the papers and so forth, and dragging up the whole Bison Tool Company business (Doris holds stock in Bison Tool but not in Multi-

Promo, which was formed in the sixties after Bobby and Doris separated), with Doris saying she had information that Bobby purposely drained the assets of Bison Tool for the benefit of Multi-Promo (or, more accurately, for the benefit of Sea Gull Management, Bobby's talent agency, a wholly owned subsidiary of Multi-Promo), and suing for damages. We have all urged Bobby to sue for divorce from Doris, because we could get plenty of evidence from members of the Kronos soccer team about Doris on the road and so forth, but Bobby hates divorce and won't go along.

The biggest difficulty has had to do with the Bobby Bison Affordables. In the late sixties (just about the time Bobby was phasing out Bison Tool as his main organization and forming Multi-Promo to facilitate his move away from hardware and so forth into service-oriented communications-based activities), Jim Trent, who was Bobby's number-one man at that time, suggested that Bobby go to various prestige locations — campuses, boutiques, discothèques — and actually *lease* a number of attractive but superfluous young people who would be obliged to do whatever Bobby asked them to do. Bobby (who, let's face it, is a very lonely man, somewhat afraid of ordinary human contact) liked the idea of a community of good-looking young people all bearing the Bobby Bison imprint and obligated to engage in all specified Bobby Bison leisure actions, so he leased several thousand "Bobby Bison Affordables."

Somehow, the Affordables never really caught on. After a while, Bobby began to try to *sublease* them to other companies, but the market just wasn't there. A certain number were able to work as servants, but the majority were just useless — and a burden on the payroll. One reason Bobby has been slow to draw up his Energy Budget for the Eighties is that he is under a lot of pressure from the "old guard" — the guys from the pre-leisure-action days, who always opposed the Affordable concept (and who got Jim Trent out of the organization) — to put the Affordables to sleep. Bobby, understandably, is reluctant to do this, because it would be an admission of failure — and the end of a dream. Still, we are all aware that the company can't go on like this, in a state of complete inaction.

Some of Bobby's early drafts for his Energy Budget for the Eighties just didn't make a lot of sense, and we had to ask Bobby to go back and try again. In one early draft, he did come up with a nice name for oil spills ("fuel-potential overages"), and in general he's been good on the whole resource-incentive area. But he keeps polishing one section, "Resentment As an Alternate Energy Source," which doesn't deal with the real problems faced at this moment by the Multi-Promo family of businesses and which inexplicably contains personal attacks on some of the people who are closest to him and who spend almost every waking hour right by his side trying to *help* him complete his energy budget.

Milo is with Bobby now. Milo has been with Bobby from the beginning, when Bison Tool was just a little shop on Erie Boulevard, and is the only one of us with any influence. Milo is going to try to get Bobby into the special exerciser and force him to come to some final decisions about his energy budget. Sometimes Milo can get Bobby into the exerciser by pretending that the straps have been disconnected, and then Bill Mandel (who hides in back of the metal understructure) jumps up and buckles down the *auxiliary* straps. It used to be that we couldn't get away with this, but recently Bobby's hair has fallen down in front of his face and he misses a lot of what goes on around him.

I Cover Carter

The Democratic Convention

Monday, July 12th, Morning

LOOKED AT U.P.I. Convention Daybook. Badly Xeroxed. Faint print. Hard to read. Thought about going to Connecticut Caucus 10 A.M. Gave it up. Thought about going to Briefing for Pages and Podium Telephone Operators. Good color. The little people, etc. etc. etc. Gave it up. Thought about going to Democratic Women's "Agenda '76" Caucus, but thought again. Decided definitely to go to Latino Caucus, West Room, Statler Hilton, but too tired.

Monday, July 12th, Afternoon

Tempted by *El Diario* Open House for Latino Delegates — good chance to brush up on Spanish for later use at later Latino caucuses, etc. etc. Decided no. Tried to sort out aspects of the New Populism (Carter's smile, etc. etc., Carter out of *nowhere,* etc. etc., possible *danger* of no political debts to Establishment, etc. etc.), but couldn't focus.

Monday, July 12th, Early Evening

Much more confident. Had a drink — one of the new Wild Turkey Old-Fashioneds people are taking up. *Found slant.* Decided to do *instant book.* Follow one crucial delegation through caucuses, etc. etc. Through floor fights. Reaction to nomination, etc. etc. Juxtapose with human interest — Amy, Miss Lillian, etc. etc. Exhausting even to think about it.

Monday, July 12th, Night

Went to Convention. Picked up credentials. Very authentic-seeming. Noticed that credentials said "News-Periphery."

Very exciting at Garden. Little electronic security devices, etc. etc. Passed security check, observed by ten or twenty members of the general public. Members of general public had no credentials. Very satisfying. Decided definitely to go ahead with instant book. Maybe on journalists — observing the observers, etc. etc. etc. Media preconceptions, etc. etc. *Altering the event.* Men of action juxtaposed with the men behind the media. *Reversed,* though. Show man behind the medium as the *true man of action,* etc. etc. Thoughtful but irreverent. Follow one team of journalists from arrival through caucuses, etc. etc. Press-room infighting, etc. etc. Print vs. electronic, etc. etc. Juxtaposed with human interest — Amy, Miss Lillian, etc. etc.

News-Periphery area very depressing. Tiny concrete bunkers. Repulsive green curtains. Clots of provincial newspersons. Worse than a game show. Worse than anything. No drinks. Very pathetic to be a newsperson. Saw one newsperson take moving pictures of a row of telephones. Very sad. One newsperson got a quote from Patrick Moynihan. On a cassette. Played it over and over. Very sad. For him. For Moynihan. For everyone. Saw a newsperson interviewing a delegate. Delegate wearing white plastic belt. Saw clot of people *training* to be newspersons. So depressing I had to sit down. Decided to skip instant book. Decided to get drink.

Bar full of foreigners. Saw Italians with leather bags. Saw Frenchmen. Nothing lower than a European newsperson. Every European had hundreds of attractive credentials. Fabulous tags reading "News-Fulcrum," "News-Podium," "News-Crucial." Not even the children had just "News-Periphery." Tried to concentrate on the *issues* — the New Constituencies, the New Credibility, the New Outsiders becoming the New *Insiders,* etc. etc. — but too depressed.

Monday, July 12th, Late Night

Went to big party. Spirits *way up*. Party given *by* staff of rock-and-roll magazine *for* staff of Jimmy Carter. Many people drinking the new Wild Turkey Old-Fashioneds, so felt right in place. Had insight, wrote it down: "Everyone here (at party) definitely born between Munich and

Yalta." Very pleased with insight. Decided to do piece about war babies molding the New Politics. The irresistible fact of *demographics*, etc. etc. Counterculture accommodations with Carter, Good Old Boys, etc. etc. Takeover generation, etc. etc. Noticed no rock-and-roll stars at party. Noticed rock-and-roll *critic*, though. Critic very upset, very *vivid*. Born about V-E Day, my guess. "Last chance to sell out," he said. "Last chance to make your deal." Afraid he'd steal my insight — war babies, etc. — so didn't say a thing.

The Campaign

September 6th

Very depressed for weeks and weeks, but *much more secure* now. Very up for in-depth campaign-diary type thing. More detail than Teddy White, etc. *More thoughtful*, too. Work in old insights — war babies, etc. Wanted to begin right away at Warm Springs, Georgia, campaign kickoff (the Roosevelt Legacy, etc. etc.), but decided better not push my luck. Almost attended Southern 500 stock-car race in Darlington, South Carolina (the Raffish South, the Unreconstructed South, etc. etc.), but decided to make diary more *selective*.

September 15th

Tried to join Carter's tour of Hans Sieverding's farm, Sioux Falls, South Dakota, but *much too far away.* Couldn't think how to even get there. Falling behind Teddy White now, I think, so a little blue.

September 23rd

Ordered big dinner, but just picked at it. Tried to watch first debate, but felt queasy. Whole thing very elusive. Might write analysis, "Elusive Politician" or "Politics of Evasion." Might not.

September 28th

Had *important insight* about Carter. Wrote it down: "Carter effectively combines virtues of Elvis Presley and Colonel Tom Parker." Not sure that's right, though. Should be *Glen Campbell* and Colonel Parker. But Colonel Parker doesn't manage Glen Campbell, so hard to sort out.

October 6th

Tried to watch second debate, but too tense. Tried to sort out Presley-Parker-Campbell image, but couldn't. *Way* behind Teddy White. Decided to do *highlights:* strong vignettes to illuminate the whole. Tried to decide *which* vignettes, but had to give it up.

October 22nd

Decided to write little essay *strongly condemning* Teddy White approach. Wrote note: "Teddy White has done for politics what Anaïs Nin has done for women." Felt very good to have written so much. Tried to watch third debate, but got the shakes and had to lie down.

October 24th

Decided on whole new angle—for *novel.* Take *one typical politician,* juxtaposed to Presidential candidate, etc. etc. *Local issues* vs. national issues, etc. etc. Similarities, *differences,* etc. etc. etc. Hopes, dreams, etc. etc. A *governor,* maybe. Only thing is, must try to figure out *which* governor.

October 26th

Found press release about a governor. So depressing I had to sit down. These people live lives you wouldn't wish on a disc jockey. Decided to write *screenplay.* Long, lonely shots (definitely use concrete bunkers from Convention, etc. etc.). One man's hopes *shattered,* etc. etc., in the midst of triumph of another man, etc. etc. etc. *Reversed, though.* Real triumph the inner growth made possible by defeat, etc. etc. etc. Human-interest figures based on Amy, Miss Lillian, etc. etc. etc. Could be big. On the other hand, could be ghastly.

November 1st

After months of thought, have definitely decided to do instant book. *Personal* approach — the election from *my hotel room.* Very pleased, because Teddy White won't have it.

November 20th

Personal approach won't work out, because *too grim.* Also worried about right hand. Right hand *won't stop shaking.* Can't write with left, so very down.

The New Administration

January 20th

Went to Inauguration. Tried to focus on whole new free spirit, but got the jitters. Tried to *lighten up,* stroll easily in the crowd, etc., but broke out in a *small red rash* (mostly on left hand) and had to go home. Best approach now: no-frills journalism. No gimmicks. Just good strong stuff. Chance to stress First One Hundred Days. *Amusing, though* — include little glossary of "cracker" terms so Washingtonians can understand Carter team, etc. etc.

February 2nd

Very down. Spotted two little "cracker" glossaries *out already*. Must do something *soon*. What about a sort of who's-who approach? Rosalynn Carter *so tough* under that sweet exterior, etc. etc. Juxtaposed to Amy, Miss Lillian, and Alice Roosevelt Longworth. Wish I knew Alice Longworth *better*. Use tape recorder for chapter on New Southern Personalities. Racist clubs, etc. etc. Almost definitely have title: "The Reign in Plains Falls Mainly on the . . ." — but can't come up with last word.

February 10th

Decided best thing go to racist club. Went to door, met by Bill. "Good evening, sir," etc. Bill said club had to let Sam go, because wanted to call members by first name. Bill said doormen, waiters, etc., at Union League Club call members by first name. Very gripping. Took mental notes. Good to be reporting again. Went upstairs, had Wild Turkey Old-Fashioned. Hand *stopped shaking*.

February 17th

See now must zero in on *energy*, Carter's plan: the new expectations, the new more modest life-styles.

April 25th

Tried to focus on energy, but too worried about *small red rash*.

May 6th

Definitely decided not to stress First One Hundred Days because too limiting. Definitely decided to forget whole New South angle because too stale. Definitely decided not to try to *lighten up* because too nervous.

July 15th

Now see must focus on *revisionist* theories. New Populism really New Conservatism. Carter Administration as caretaker government, Carter as apostle of closed government, Carter as savior of Northern élite. Ordered big lunch, but couldn't get it down. Decided small red rash definitely *spreading*.

Mrs. Armand Reef Likes to Entertain

JOANNE REEF, just thirty, just divorced, curls up in a tiny chintz chair in her East Side flat and talks about her life as a hostess. Around her tiny chair, on the floor, there are big red jars with no labels, which contain various oils and essences (vegetable pulp, compressed ripening gels, mineral suspensions) which have a role in the preparation of the "Over-All Body Dew" she will be marketing soon under her own name. One lock of her famous red hair is tucked easily into her mouth. "I lead a quiet life," she says. "I must have time to work on my formulas, you see, to perfect my Body Dew and my new Neutral Eyeliner, and I insist on having time for my children, because, of course, I adore them — my children — and I think they are so wise, children, and one can learn so much."

Joanne Reef is silent for a moment. Slowly, almost reluctantly, she turns her attention to the question of her evening entertainments. "It is true that I have not lost faith in the small dinner party," she says at last.

Joanne Reef *wants* to be open, to talk frankly, but she holds back. With some slight trace of nervousness, she moves her foot, causing a small noise of chintz. Because

I want to earn her trust I do not ask about her ex-husband, socialite-sportsman Armand Reef, or her father, Arnold Sworf, indicted proprietor of the Midlothian Resort Spa chain of leisure hotels. I ask her what she thinks about entertaining on a large scale. I ask her if there is room today for the *grand service:* tiny songbirds at each place (alive at first), fine china made from crushed bone, ejection, mockery, vivid Hungarian music.

"No, no," she says firmly. "I think that the public will hardly put up with that sort of thing now. No, I do not think we shall see those days again. I feel almost certain that now it is the small dinner party that is at the cutting edge."

Now Joanne Reef is more relaxed, more trusting. "My list is small — very small really," she says. "Just a few old friends and a very few 'new people,' principally from the arts and politics. There are no hard-and-fast rules, but I will be honest. To be asked to one of my little dinner parties you must have great intelligence. And wit. I value wit. I love the clever thing — the thing that just *glances off* the truth and circles back to something topical. I am crushed if my guests are not able to speak easily to one another (and to me!) in the language of intelligence and wit."

In changing positions in her chair, Joanne Reef knocks over one of the big red jars, spilling a clear viscous fluid (one of the ripening gels) over the carpet. She is not upset, she says, because her floor covering is made from densely woven natural fibers from the north of Canada, which have the ability to absorb liquid. Indeed, after only a moment, the viscous fluid disappears, leaving nothing more than an aura of damp resilience.

Mrs. Reef takes a small sip of a mixed drink made with Ultra Vodka, a brand she is helping to make popular. After a moment she is willing to discuss some of the controversial aspects of her parties. She says that it is true that she prefers to invite high-powered men and cheap women. "I find that high-powered dynamic men like to humiliate easy women, and that makes a party *go*," she says frankly. She reveals that she often gives to the dynamic men she invites some special little gift — a little cushion, perhaps, with personalized decoration done in appliqué. She admits that she gives no little gifts to her women guests. "The only way a woman can get a little cushion is if one of the dynamic men gives her one," she explains. "This happens from time to time, but not often. Dynamic men like to *keep* their cushions, I find — for naps or for other reasons. Sometimes, though, the powerful men at my dinners insert their little cushions *under the hips* of the cheap women, which is sweet, I think."

A small figure, very vague in outline, looks in at the door of the room where we are sitting. Mrs. Reef says that it is one of her children. "I am preoccupied with my children," she says. "Almost overly so." She describes one of her children as "very small," and the other as "somewhat larger." I ask which child it was that appeared at the door. "That one looked very small," she says.

A moment later, a larger, more definite figure enters the room. This is Albert Morm, Joanne Reef's partner and business manager.

"I want you to know Albert," Joanne Reef says. "He is a very remarkable person."

Albert Morm pours himself a cocktail, made with Ultra Vodka. "What we're doing with Over-All Body Dew is giving today's woman a chance to opt for complete moisturization," Albert Morm says.

"What I love is this new Ultra Vodka," Joanne Reef says.

"What we're not going to do is blow Joanne's credibility by having her involved in every damn thing that comes down the pike," Albert Morm says.

"I could have made a *fortune*," Joanne Reef says vehemently.

"And blown your image down the tubes," says Albert Morm. Morm leans forward and looks intently at me. "Joanne is the most contemporary person I know," he says. "Her name will be associated with a very small number of important products which reflect her personal concerns and life-style."

Shifting rapidly in her chair, Joanne Reef knocks over a red jar full of vegetable pulp. The pulp cannot be seen clearly against the floor covering.

"See that — that's *Tundra,*" says Albert Morm, indicating the carpet. "A million-dollar idea."

"Shut up, Al, and make me a drink," Joanne Reef says.

After a while Mr. Morm leaves, and Joanne and I find ourselves alone — quiet, almost *close.* We both take a small cocktail, made with Ultra Vodka. "Don't think it's all so Goddamned easy," she says at last. "Sometimes I'm short of guests and I have to call up the Bureau of Labor Statistics and have them send someone over; and sometimes they're all booked, and it's too late to call anyone else, and I just give up and cancel."

Joanne Reef gets out of her chair and grinds the toe of her shoe into the Tundra floor covering. "*In which case,*" she says, looking with satisfaction as a few drops of the spilled ripening gel rise to the surface, "I take all the stemware from the table and drop it item by item from my bedroom window."

Gerry Plume Does Her Own Commercials

I APPROACHED THE SET — a corduroy sofa and a cocktail table placed out on the boardwalk, near the rail. Beyond camera range were a keno game and a shop selling enormous towels. I waited for Gerry Plume, estranged wife of Stanley Plume (the real-estate magnate, now gravely ill). She arrived — a small figure in an orange pants suit. She smiled.

"Do you like my smile?" she asked disarmingly. "I was so afraid to smile. For years and years. When you are a little girl, you see, and someone says 'No,' or 'Don't,' or 'I think you look like nothing at all,' you lose a little bit of your smile." Suddenly, Gerry Plume began to cry. The technicians on the set did not seem to notice, but people from the keno game looked over in curiosity. Gerry looked back, smiling. "It's only that I'm so happy that I do my own commercials now," she told me.

The filming began. The script (written by Gerry, in collaboration with a male friend named Sal and her companion/secretary, a tall woman of middle age named Miss Sweedie) called for Gerry to lie face down on the corduroy sofa, as though asleep, and then to spring up as though prodded by an electric shock, and then to talk rapidly about the sofa. This happened. Then Sal, dressed in a very abbreviated bathing suit, walked by. Then Sal came to sit by Gerry on the sofa and seemed to be interested in her for a while. Then he lost interest and fell asleep on the sofa. At this point, Miss Sweedie came in, dressed in a nurse's uniform. Miss Sweedie took Gerry firmly by the arm. "Time for your shot," she said. Then Gerry looked over at Sal asleep on the sofa and threw up her arms in mock despair. "Gerry Plume Adult Divans, Did You Have To Be That Comfortable?" she said.

A crowd had wandered over from the keno game to watch the filming. One man, with a small goatee and a luxuriant head of tightly curled hair, stayed behind when the filming was over. A short blond woman urged him to leave. "This is just nothing," the blond woman said.

"I've seen it on TV," the man said. "The Gerry Plume Adult Divans."

Gerry Plume turned to the man. "Bless you," she said.

I talked to Gerry. She was radiant. "I am going to be honest with you," she said. "Until my husband had his stroke, I was a nobody. Oh, I had all the *position,* all the *prestige.* I mean, I didn't have to play frontsies-backsies to cut the line at Vegas or what have you, or *Tahoe* or what have you. But *inside* I felt just like nothing at all."

I asked how she came to be involved in the sofa business.

"It was a small foreclosure action," she said, taking a long, thin cigarette from what looked like a custom-made tortoiseshell case. "It's a Delaware corporation, but the goods are made in Korea from something *shredded.* I forget just what. But whatever it is, they have to process it quite a lot, and there was one batch they didn't process *quite enough* and the police impounded it and then they began to have cash-flow problems and so we loaned them some money on *very favorable terms* and about a month later the government ruled that the stuff they impounded was dangerous to children and had to be shipped back to Korea, and then we took over."

I asked Gerry how she had managed to keep her goods from being shipped back to Korea, and then Miss Sweedie came over to where we were standing. She put herself between us, her back to me. "Time for your shot," she said to Gerry.

"Oh, Miss Sweedie, not during my *interview,*" Gerry said almost plaintively.

"Time for your shot," Miss Sweedie said.

I wandered down the boardwalk. The boardwalk was saturated with an oily preservative used to retard decay. Small articles of litter were trapped by the oily preservative in a way that clogged the drainage holes and caused small oily puddles. Through lack of attention, I walked into an oily puddle.

"That'll penetrate right through," a voice said. I turned and saw the man with the luxuriant hair. "Might as well rip them up and throw them away," he said, looking me straight in the eye. I walked on, ignoring him. He fell into step. "What we do, we wear special shoes," he said. Without meaning to, I looked at his shoes. They seemed to be made out of a fragment of snow tire. They had giant rubber treads. "In spring, when they're laying the stuff down, the puddles get real bad, but the special shoes will go straight on through — no problem," he said.

Suddenly he stopped. "This is where I work," he said. He was standing in front of an amusement ride called the Tyke Track. Small mockups of cars from the nineteen-fifties were attached to a moving chain that pulled them around an elevated course. The chain slackened at times, and the cars lurched forward uncertainly at erratic speeds. Small children, many in their infancy, were fastened, and sometimes lashed, to the steering wheels. "It's kind of like a day-care thing," the man said. "The kids stay on pretty near all day. Some of them get pretty dizzy."

I began to walk back to the set. "I should be on television, some of the things that happen to *me*," the man shouted as I walked away.

Back at the set, I found that Gerry Plume had stepped

in a puddle. The oily preservative had penetrated the cuffs of her pants. But she knew just where she had left off. "To make a long story short, I found out that we could use the shredded material if we certified we wouldn't sell to children," she said. "That was when I came up with the Gerry Plume Adult Divans concept with the accent on adult pleasure."

She smiled, and then suddenly she got up and went over toward the keno game, where Miss Sweedie was standing. Gerry's movements were staccato.

Miss Sweedie looked sullen. "Keep your distance," she shouted as Gerry approached her.

Gerry came back. Her sense of balance seemed to be off. She seemed to be glad to sit down. "Miss Sweedie is very upset because I ruined my pants," Gerry said. She took another long cigarette out of her case. "So *then* we began to promote and promote and promote, which is the name of the game, as you know, and we began to think more and more in terms of a TV campaign — local stations, late night — and my husband began to audition these girls — models and so forth. And, of course, like an *idiot,* I didn't even have the sense to *object,* let alone think of *myself.* But then, thank God, my husband had his stroke and we were stuck, and so *Sal* said, 'Why don't you do it, Gerry? You're the best-looking woman in New York' — which is *absurd,* of course, but Sal *is* very supportive. So, to make a long story short, we just began to *fool around* — Sal and Miss Sweedie and myself — with no idea that it would work, until I came up with the 'Gerry Plume Adult Divans, Did You Have To Be That Comfortable?' concept and the whole thing just took off."

I looked over toward the keno game and saw that the man with the luxuriant hair had come back. He stood just beyond the set. He began to move forward, but Miss Sweedie stuck out her foot and he tripped. He got up. He cupped his hands around his mouth. "Just keep it up — you're beautiful," he shouted at Gerry.

"Bless you," Gerry shouted back.

"You're beautiful," the man shouted, very excited.

"You're beautiful," Gerry shouted back.

"You're a beautiful person," the man shouted.

"I just wish I could get this crap off my pants," Gerry said.

I rode back to the city with Gerry. Sal drove. I sat in back with Gerry and Miss Sweedie. Gerry sat in the middle. "Believe me, I've been through the whole *routine*," she said. "*House*, children, husband, husband, husband. Up to my ears."

"Now he's in intensive care," Sal said, turning his head halfway around, so that he was looking neither at the road nor at us.

"*I* was in intensive care for seventeen years," Gerry said. "And how." The car pulled off the highway. "Turn your back," Gerry said. I turned my back and looked out the window. We were driving through a grid of houses built during the twenties or thirties on land abutting an oil refinery. I felt Gerry writhing in the seat next to me. At one moment, both her buttocks rested awkwardly on my right arm. "O.K. to look," she said. I looked and saw that she had taken off her orange pants suit and put on a little tennis outfit. She held the top of her pants suit in her lap. Miss Sweedie had the bottoms. "That's the trouble with synthetics," Gerry said. "They just sop up anything oily."

The car came to a stop in front of a small house. It was strangely narrow. It had a front porch that looked as though it were only big enough for two people. Miss Sweedie got out of the car, taking the pants. She went up onto the porch of the house. Miss Sweedie nearly filled the porch. The door opened and a woman looked out. Miss Sweedie threw the pants at the woman in the doorway. "We decided to give the stained part to my sister," Gerry said. "It was Miss Sweedie's idea." Gerry turned to look at me. "Miss Sweedie has a very nice side. She really has."

We drove to Gerry's tennis club. "It just makes you feel like so much more of a person to have people recognize you and so forth," Gerry said. "And service. People recognize you and you get much better service. When I think of the years I wasted." Gerry was silent for a moment. Suddenly she turned to me — almost violently. "I'll tell you something," she said. "If you ever get a chance to do something like what I'm doing — my own commercials — grab it. I tried everything. I did the whole bit. Philanthropy. Everything. I was the first one to organize for blindness in my building. It got me nowhere, exactly nowhere. Now — I'm in on the tennis boom, you name it."

Gerry, as though exhausted, sat back in the seat. "Time for your shot," Miss Sweedie said. Gerry shook her head. "Not before *sports*," Gerry said.

"Time for your shot," Miss Sweedie said.

Gerry looked at me wearily. "Turn your back," she said.

Rated

"Coming Near to You" is rated in a certain way because of some fairly routine violence. No problem. No problem. The problem of violence is not a problem. Routine violence is routine — so routine that it's no real problem, no real threat. When the man shows the wound on his chest, there is no problem. When the other man smiles at the wound on the man's chest, there is no problem. When the woman takes snapshots of the wound and encourages others to smile, there is no problem, even when the pictures, the snaps, hundreds of them, are sold on the streets, on the corners, in the places where people stand and wait, where children stand and wait. No problem. The opposite of a problem. The negative outline of a problem, a *joke* on a problem. No slowdown or holdup, no obstacle to everyone's seeing and liking it — the wound, the smile at the wound, the reproduction of the wound, and the smiles and distribution. No problem.

Some people will take a test, that's all. Selected people will sit quietly and see *Coming Near to You,* and then they will sit quietly and take a little test. They will come to a room we have set aside. They will come in the side entrance, through the marble rotunda that was so expensive to build — oh, years ago, when we believed in marble and rotundas, when we liked the way feet sounded against polished floors. People will be led in the side door because during the hours we give the tests the main entrance is closed. How we used to love it, the main entrance! How we used to love it, the main screen! And not just the main screen — tall as a private building — but the *gold tent* that used to spread or seem to spread out from the space above the screen, that used to spread above the screen and protect it, each fold distinct — how we used to love it! But people now come in another way, see another set of details. People now are led to a basement area that is very secure, and they stay there awhile, that's all. They wait for a while; they wait long enough for an edge of distance to form, that's all. Then they answer a few questions, because we want to know how they feel. We want to know how people feel when the women amputate the foot of the dead man. It is routine, the amputation, but we want to know if people feel the need for it. Did it seem well motivated? Was there a need for the camera to hover on the severing, in terms of the development of the theme of separation, etc. etc., the theme of bad news, etc. etc., the emphasis on awkward movement, etc. etc.? And the romance. Was the romance upsetting? We want to know that. Some groups — groups of girls with short hair done in a little flip, *cheerful* girls — might find the romance upsetting. And the background. Some people might find that upsetting — streets where there are people with parts elongated or compressed, shaped out of the normal.

We've asked every sort of person. We've gone right up. We ask them every kind of question. Sometimes they don't want to answer, but not too often. We follow them to their homes. We sit down to talk honestly: "Do you honestly feel that it was well motivated, the way people on the street were compressed and elongated and shaped out of the normal? Was it an essential element in the forward movement of the plot?" Some people don't have the wit to answer honestly. The education they have! Nothing. They barely know their own name. We ask again and again. "Is that really your name?" we ask. We ask to see three pieces of identification. Driver's license, major-department-store charge card, and something from their church. Then we say, "Thank you," because we are polite and serious, and then we do follow-up work, after the special showing.

After the special showing, we empty the theatre row by row. That's the way we do it. Row A, Row B, etc. etc. Then we can measure the stress. We watch them very closely. Sometimes when it comes to a written test, people are very shy about admitting that they were under stress — "Doesn't make any difference to me what shape people are," they say — but if you watch, their hand trembles a little and the movement of their eye is a little out of the normal, and all that can be monitored if you are careful and empty the theatre row by row.

We know *Coming Near to You* produces stress. Row after row, these people in the theatre were under stress. People in the theatre were under stress watching people in the film. We know it. The woman named Jaycinette, for instance — she was under stress. And people *in* the film. Some of the people *in* the film, *paid* to be in the film, the dress extras and so forth — some of these people seemed upset to be exposed to what was going on. They were under stress, you could tell. Jaycinette was under stress, you could tell. She took her pencil and gouged the point deep into her test. She put her hand to her neck and twisted her necklace just like the people in the movie when they were under stress. Like Sally Herley. Miss Herley, who is doing so well, who will do anything, anything on film, and not complain — she was under stress, you could tell. Jaycinette, in the perfectly comfortable interview situation where she had to spend a little time — Jaycinette put her hand to her neck just the way Sally Herley did in the movie. It was the same thing. Jaycinette was wearing a necklace — that was the only difference. Jaycinette had a necklace spelling out "Jaycinette" in an inexpensive gold-tone material — that was the only difference. It spelled out "Jaycinette" when she kept her hands quiet, but under stress she twisted the necklace and it didn't make any sense at all. That was the only difference.

Coming Near to You had to be rated in a certain way because of the stress. With all that stress, *Coming Near to You,* despite the hope at the end, the way people crawl back on top and wave, the way they fit their shapes together and wave, the way the music comes on so you don't notice the problems in the theatre, the shredded fabric on the seats, etc., the falling plaster, etc. etc. — despite the hope at the end, it had to be rated in a certain way.

• THREE •

At Lunch with the Rock Critic Establishment

I WENT TO LUNCH with the Rock Critic Establishment. No one said anything about its being a lunch for the Rock Critic Establishment. No one was as unsubtle as that. Nonetheless, all of us at lunch knew that we constituted the Rock Critic Establishment, as how could we not?

Vivian Aspair was there. Vivian Aspair is the editor of *Mother Rock*, the feminist rock-and-roll quarterly. Vivian has a theory that women have an innate urge toward percussion which has been thwarted by men. Vivian Aspair is trouble. Vivian Aspair tries for effect, always, and clings to an outmoded preference for 45-r.p.m. singles. She used to live with Lester Rax, but that was before Monterey. She drinks Wild Turkey, which is something she picked up from the Allman Brothers Band.

Havana and Dominica Davenport (who are Negroes) arrived together. They walked right by Vivian and sat down next to Lester Rax. Havana and Dominica cultivate Lester Rax. It was Lester who gave Havana and Dominica their first break in *Moonshadows* magazine (the old *Moonshadows*, the monthly on newsprint, not the slick faggot weekly that comes out now). Dominica, who hates textiles of any kind, was wearing aluminum party pants, as usual. Havana was dressed in a soft feminine caftan but wore one of the little metal spiders people are taking up.

"I love your spider," Lester Rax said to Havana.

Anson Briggs, who was the first person to describe Elton John as "annoying," spoke to Vivian but not to Lester Rax, and not, thus, to Dominica or Havana Davenport. Anson and Lester have never been close, although both of them are friends of David Gorm, the most important of the daily critics. David and Anson and Lester go to the same exercise class, but they are assigned to different platoons. Anson Briggs, in talking to Vivian Aspair, tried to turn the conversation to 45-r.p.m. singles. Anson told Vivian that he had all the singles Elvis put out on Sun.

Vivian laughed wickedly. "That's just pathetic," she said. "That's the most pathetic thing I ever heard in my life." Vivian laughed again.

People grew silent to hear Vivian's laugh.

"He's got all the Elvis singles on Sun," Vivian said loudly. "Him and five million shopgirls."

Lester Rax just ignored Vivian. It really gets to Vivian when Lester ignores her. Sometimes when the Rock Critic Establishment comes together all that really happens is that Lester ignores Vivian and then Vivian makes so much trouble Lester can't ignore her anymore and then the group breaks up. Lester is the most important member of the Rock Critic Establishment. It is impossible to forget that Lester founded the old *Moonshadows* magazine on National Merit Scholarship money. But Lester offends a lot of people. Jack Loam, a very thoughtful writer, doesn't talk to Lester. Angela Farl, another writer of distinction, quarrelled with Lester over "Blood on the Tracks," and Lester was so incredibly mean about it that she moved to Dallas. Writers like Trinc in Boston, Halstin in L.A., and Joppe, Sloan, and Hawthorn (from the old *Polecat* group in San Francisco) steer clear of Lester altogether.

To one side (at lunch) stood Mary Jacro, who is not a member of the Rock Critic Establishment. Mary Jacro writes for the leisure pages of an important news weekly. She goes to concerts all the time, which none of the rest of us really do — except for Gorm. Mary Jacro will interview anyone. Once she found herself on a hydrofoil with Jim Morrison, but nothing came of it. Mary Jacro brought to lunch a friend who was a researcher for her news weekly. This researcher thought that Mary Jacro belonged to the Rock Critic Establishment.

"Isn't that Vivian Aspair?" the researcher asked.

"Oh, yes," said Mary Jacro.

"Do you know Vivian Aspair?" asked the researcher.

"Oh, yes," said Mary Jacro. "We went through the whole Isle of Wight thing together."

"Why don't you *talk* to her?" asked the researcher.

"No one talks much at these things," said Mary Jacro, cursing the little researcher to herself.

Lunch for the Rock Critic Establishment was provided by the publicity department of Modern Rhythm Records. Allison Fradrer, the head of Artist Development at Modern Rhythm Records, supervised the catering. The vogue at that moment was for very expensive lunches. There was saddle of lamb, there were tiny little carrots and tiny little potatoes, and there were several wines.

"Oh, God," said Lester Rax. "Saddle of lamb again." Lester Rax took on his plate the tiny carrots only.

Vivian Aspair began to pound her thigh with her fist in a manner that was percussive.

"Oh, God," said Lester Rax. "Vivian is going into one of her trances."

Allison Fradrer handed out press kits. The vogue at that moment was for press kits with a piece of clothing inside. Each press kit contained a flannel shirt. The flannel shirts were white. Across each one the legend "TRAITOR" had been stencilled in black. Allison tried to talk for a minute to each member of the Rock Critic Establishment as she handed out the press kits. She gave extra time to Lester Rax. She told Lester about the rock-and-roll group Traitor.

"Listen, I wouldn't try to hype you, Les," she began. "I mean, let's talk turkey — these kids aren't really traitors. I mean, Jimmy, the lead, spent some time in

Sweden, and I think he was involved in some fragging or something, but we're really not even pushing that angle."

"Good," Lester said.

"The other kids — Rushing, Jake, and Calvin — have just had the usual drug busts and I think we're just going to soft-pedal the whole thing," Allison said.

"Great," Lester said.

"I told them upstairs, 'Don't hype it with a criminal-record thing, because it will just backfire,' " Allison said. "And so we're going with a much more honest approach, which is great because we don't really *need* to hype it, because in *spirit* these kids are *completely* criminal and against the whole blind-loyalty-duty-sin-guilt thing."

"Umm," Lester said.

"Which is *exactly* where it's at," Allison said. "I mean, *beyond* Punk Rock."

"Beyond Punk Rock?" Vivian asked wickedly. "Did she say '*beyond* Punk Rock'?"

"I'm sorry, Allison," Lester said. "I think it's just hype."

"Oh, no," Allison said.

"This kid Calvin," Lester said. "Wasn't he . . . didn't he . . . do backup for Donovan?"

"He was a *child*," Allison said. "My God, you can't hold that against him. And he was very disillusioned. He practically had a breakdown. It was *very painful*." Allison was nervous. Everyone else was quiet — even Vivian.

"I'm sorry, Allison," Lester said. "I'm afraid it's just hype."

I should explain that Lester has the most stringent standards of anyone in the Rock Critic Establishment. Some people think that because he usually goes to the Coast on the Modern Rhythm jet his position has been compromised, but it isn't true. Lester won't lie for anybody. Lester was the first to say that Jimi Hendrix was being too self-indulgent with those endless riffs. "The ultimate groove is one chord, but so what?" was something Lester said. He said that to Ben Joppe at a time when Joppe was deep into Cream and Cream was deep into jamming. Lester has always said exactly what was on his mind. Lester has always stood for complete integrity. Where Lester goes wrong is that he doesn't know his own power. The fact is that the Rock Critic Establishment is an enormously powerful institution, and the fact is that Lester is the most powerful member of that institution. But Lester just won't come to terms with that.

Allison Fradrer gave a Traitor shirt to Mary Jacro. Allison treats Mary Jacro as though she were a member of the Rock Critic Establishment, which is why Modern Rhythm gets coverage in the leisure pages of Mary Jacro's news weekly. Allison Fradrer gave a shirt to Mary Jacro's friend, the little researcher. The researcher put the shirt on right then and there, which was a big gaffe and very embarrassing to Mary Jacro. To make up for the researcher's gaffe and to make sure she stayed on the Modern Rhythm guest list (and to make sure she got another chance to meet Vivian Aspair), Mary Jacro promised Allison Fradrer a spread on Traitor in the leisure pages of her news weekly. (This spread, by the way, saved Allison Fradrer's job. Allison had been in deep trouble for failing to get any coverage for the comeback of Valerian DiMucci, who is doing disco versions of his 1956 hits, with no success at all. Allison staged a shooting for Traitor at the old immigration depot on Ellis Island, and Mary Jacro wrote a story under the headline "TRAITOR: BEYOND PUNK ROCK." This story, the only publicity resulting from the Traitor lunch, was then made into a little flyer, which was reproduced in quantity and sent to the members of the Rock Critic Establishment, who threw it away.)

Gerald Shine arrived for dessert, which was a very delicate *mousse au citron*. Gerald Shine is *indirectly* a member of the Rock Critic Establishment. He writes a column for a mimeographed tip sheet. What he does, mostly, is write about members of the Rock Critic Establishment. Gerald Shine is the only person who is on speaking terms with both Vivian and Lester. Gerald sat down next to Vivian Aspair, and just at that minute Jimmy Garvin, the lead singer of Traitor, came in. Allison Fradrer had hoped Jimmy Garvin wouldn't come to lunch, but it was hard to explain to him why he shouldn't come, so he came. Gerald Shine looked at Jimmy Garvin with contempt.

"Well, what do we think of *this* number?" Gerald asked Vivian Aspair.

"Just Ticketron trash," said Vivian Aspair.

"Oh!" said Gerald Shine with mock horror. "Aren't you *mean*."

Lester talked to Havana Davenport about real estate. Lester predicted continued softness in the condominium market. Allison Fradrer waited for Lester to finish. Then, very politely, she asked Lester if he would like to meet Jimmy Garvin, the lead singer of Traitor.

"That's very sweet of you to ask," Lester said. "But no."

It was a mistake for Allison to go to Lester first. If there had been a *major* star in the room, protocol would have demanded that he be brought to Lester first, but it was a mistake to bring, or even to offer to bring, a *non-established* singer to Lester first. If Lester had agreed to meet Jimmy Garvin it would have seemed like an endorsement, since the meeting would have taken place in front of the entire Rock Critic Establishment. So Lester was obliged to refuse. Allison Fradrer had the sense to know that once Lester had refused to meet Jimmy Garvin everyone else in the Rock Critic Establishment would refuse to meet him, too, so she took Jimmy Garvin over to Mary Jacro and the little researcher. Mary Jacro was thrilled. The little researcher, who had been having doubts, was convinced that Mary Jacro belonged to the Rock Critic Establishment after all.

Gerald Shine was angry that he had not been given a chance to refuse to meet Jimmy Garvin, the lead singer of Traitor. To show how annoyed he was he went up to Lester Rax and told Lester that he thought Traitor was going to be big. "I think they're going to happen, Les," he said. "I really do. I love the whole disloyalty thing. I think it's very new. I think it's the most exciting thing since Anson discovered Bruce Springsteen."

This was just an incredibly explosive thing for Gerald Shine to say, and it brought up the most complicated and *dangerous* issues facing the Rock Critic Establishment. Actually, Trinc had been the first writer to see Springsteen: Trinc saw Springsteen and told Ben Joppe that Springsteen was "great," and then Joppe saw Springsteen and said Springsteen was "great," too. But Trinc and Joppe are into a whole *reportorial* number, and while they are respected, they aren't really *critics,* and they see hundreds of singers and they say So-and-So is "great" and it doesn't matter so much. So it wasn't until a month or so after Joppe said Springsteen was "great" in the Sunday *Times* entertainment section that it really began to happen. What happened was that Lester began to feel that it was time for him to get involved, and he saw Springsteen and began to write a really long piece, which everyone knew about and was waiting for, but in the meantime Anson Briggs saw Springsteen and had a *minor stroke* at the performance, which got a lot of publicity, and when Anson Briggs returned to consciousness he said that he had had a vision of Springsteen as a Black Angel and he said that Springsteen "justified the future," which was a phrase that caught on. So Briggs got all the credit for discovering Springsteen, which was ironic, because the piece that Lester wrote about Springsteen was probably the finest thing he ever did and was a beautiful piece of writing.

Lester was cool in the face of Gerald Shine's hostile remark. "I think that's just hype, Gerald" was what Lester said. It really annoyed Gerald that Lester was so cool, and he left without finishing his *mousse au citron.* Vivian was really mad, too. She came up to Havana Davenport, who was sitting right next to Lester. "I just hate your stupid metal spider," she said, and then she left, and the party thinned out.

There has been an incredible amount of malicious talk about what happened at lunch that day, most of it started by Gerald Shine. I have heard people say that Lester threw a metal spider at Vivian, that Lester made a pass at Mary Jacro, that Lester tried to punch out Anson Briggs, and so on, but none of that is true. The most stupid rumor was that Lester tried to get Jimmy Garvin, lead singer of Traitor, to pose for nude pictures, which is completely untrue, and which shows that some people still confuse Lester Rax with Lester Walkib, the

Syrian who is the editor of the new *Moonshadows* magazine. Later on, Lester Walkib did take some pictures of Jimmy Garvin for the new *Moonshadows,* but he wasn't at lunch that day (that day, in fact, he was presenting the Walkib Dance Award to an octogenarian ballerina), and in any case he is definitely not a member of the Rock Critic Establishment — a fact that must irk him.

Q & A

A: Would you like your chair moved closer? Would you like a little pillow? Would you like to see my film again?

Q: I'm very comfortable. With you. With the film. With the special chair. I have been comfortable right from the start. Almost from the start. I was comfortable with my hope to meet you. I was comfortable with your name in my datebook. I was comfortable when we drove to the Valley.

A: Shall we scan the promotional literature? Would you like to snap my picture?

Q: You took me out in your car. Through the hills, along those winding roads where the baby stars live, to the Valley. The drive — so like you, Sammy. The man of myth. The man who stood outside the big hotels dressed in velvet with his guitar and *that smile*, just a wreath of insight on his lips (which opened in such a way, to such an extent, that even the police took notice) — you like to drive in the Valley. Enfolding yourself in a sense of American nowhere. An arrangement of silence, perhaps, so your thoughts can have their outline.

Your feet are very large. It was practically the first

thing I noticed. From years on the road your feet have bloomed — have absorbed some mineral from the pavement and spread to an enormous width. I wanted to see your feet up close, without the shoes, but I was too shy to ask.

In the Valley, the air seemed to hang just above the second story. Two-story commercial entities supporting the low sky. We have learned to respect commercial things, the things we have come to perceive as artifacts. They support the low California sky! The laundromats, where the people converge for an exchange of anxious glances within the context of homely work; the shops with a religious aim; the machines dispensing drinks. And the little gaps where a shop has gone away, been erased. You know these things are the great American things!

You stopped the car and got out. You seemed not to notice me. That way it was much more real, had much more impact. You went into a small shop that turned out to be an amusement center — one of the artifacts we have come to respect. There were dozens of pinball machines lined against a wall. The wall itself was fragile, made of paper pressed together by a steaming process. The layers of wall buckle, then come free, like petals from a bud, because the process is unreliable. A lasting adhesion is not sought. The layers of paper, springing apart, present a surface in tiers, like a cross-section of skin. Without a word, you left. I was alone in the amusement center, which I had not expected. For a while I didn't move, because I thought you might want me to keep still. Then I intended to move, saw a moving figure that was the figure of my intention stride away, down a line of pinball machines (touching a finger to the glass case of each in sequence to preserve an attitude of interest, which is my attitude at times), and out the door. But I did not move. I kept still, in case you wanted me to. My comfort was in my observation of the line of pinball machines, which comprised many machines but only one game, the game called "Recent Scores," after your great song. I located my attitude of interest and noticed it peel away, revealing you. You are large. On the game boards under the glass your head is large. Your hair curls down to a special lane where it is possible to trap a ball. You hold a guitar, of course, and just above the guitar there are five drop targets. Around the targets float three feminine figures, disguised for legal purposes (because you don't want to cut them in on the royalties) but still emerging as Star Murley, Sally Molloy, and Lilly Pol, the women of your songs. Just below the five drop targets there is another drop target, placed in such a way that it is very difficult to hit, given the arc described by the flippers. The single drop target lights the double-bonus feature and is surrounded by a beautiful representation of Dearie, your young daughter by Sally Molloy.

I waited a long time for you to come back, but you didn't come. After a while an employee of the amusement center brought me a cool drink, and then a bowl of cereal. I stayed the night. It is embarrassing to wait for you, but it is a little exciting, too. You are elusive — everyone knows that. Sometimes you agree to an appointment. I make the appointment with your personal manager — an ex-convict who got out of prison because you wrote a song about him, who is seen with two young girls, one black and one white, always, who earns more money than any politician — and I come to the office of this man at a certain hour, and you don't show up. I wait and wait and wait with your personal manager. I notice that there are no letters or papers on his desk, no writing of any kind. Then it gets embarrassing in a way that is exciting, because of the yielding quality, and then it gets so embarrassing that I have to go home.

I went home. I listened to your songs. Sometimes when you don't show up and I have to go home, I listen to your songs so much it makes me sweat. I can remember with perfect clarity the first time I heard you sing. I was nobody. I was just a nothing. When I think of the clothes I used to wear, and the eyeglasses — gray plastic as thick as glue around the huge lenses, weighing down on my small nose — I just laugh and laugh! The song was "See Pain." Of course, by then you had already released two albums. How was I to know, in the place where I was? "See Pain" was from the "Tethered" album. The cover of that album — you, so young, your head bent, hair cut short, *that smile* directed to the pavement where your feet were beginning to spread (from days on the road, Michigan to Carmine Alley to Chicago, where the

Negro singers were, and back) — that picture of you had been seen and had made its mark, but I didn't know.

Sometimes when you want to talk to somebody, you send a convict — one of the convicts you set free with your songs, who are in your employ, who go on tour, who earn more money than any politician. Sometimes you send a girlfriend — an old girlfriend, one of the minor girlfriends, not one from the songs. These girls hit the lounges where the writers go — desperate writers too lacking in confidence to call your personal manager. They are forward, these girls. They keep quarters in the old bungalow colonies, the ones built in the twenties. At times, a whole bungalow colony is filled with these girls, each with a writer, giving you your choice. Sometimes, toward dawn, there is the sound of your footfall from window to window. Then, as morning comes, you break into a bungalow and give an interview. Gerry Trinc got the story on the "Nest Lease" tapes that way. Poor Trinc, so sad toward the end — his ears shrivelled and dead, his eyes blinded by glare, all his senses diminished from years at the big halls. You sent a girl to get Trinc and you gave him the story, when Lester Rax and so many others were keeping still in the office of your personal manager. The whole story — the legendary sessions you made in a secret basement space with just a pickup band, those blond men who had never come in from the road, who just toured and toured, absorbing the minerals from the pavement, setting up in abandoned gas stations, small clothing stores, anywhere out of sight — that story, of secret music made by secret men, you gave to Trinc. Appeared at the door and told it to him straight.

Sally Molloy came to my door. As simple as that. Sally has lost a lot of weight. All the long hair that you wrote about is gone. Her hair is done in a little flip now, which is much too cheerful. I went with her, of course.

Sally said, "The feeling now is that it's ridiculous to talk about the form the film has taken. Now the feeling is that it was a booming energy going in many directions. We've treated it like a fine horse. Given it a pace. Sammy says the film is like that."

We drove down the boulevard past the bungalow colonies, where I knew there were other writers with other girls. Sally drove me to your big metal house and showed me through the rooms.

The first room resembled the upper Middle West — vast and very lonely, from that time in your life. Sally said, "There was a feeling that there should be a space to represent the space that Sammy left. We had Lester Rax working on the script for a while, but then we had to let him go, because there was a feeling that a script was too much like punctuation. I drove him to the station. He cried and cried, but he had to go. But he had this idea that there should be a space to represent the space that Sammy left, and Sammy kept that idea in." I noticed a sign in a frame — a hand-carved frame, like little logs notched together. The sign listed the few objects in the vast room, which were original objects from your early life, including the wrappers you put on your schoolbooks to keep them fresh.

"This room was Lester's dream and Lester's comfort before he had to leave," said Sally Molloy. "Lester used to come here for hours and stand completely still, just like he was part of the landscape. Not moving at all, in case Sammy wanted it that way. It was done for love." I stood close to Sally, and she let me stand close to her for a minute but then she moved away. "You can stand close to me if you want, but it won't mean a thing," she said.

Sally took me into the room that is a reconstruction of the attic where you lived in Carmine Alley, where you slept on the floor with your head in the crook of your arm. There was a typed description of the room in a log frame, and I read it, and then there was a scream, like the sound of someone in enormous pain. It was hard to assess the quality of the pain. Recently, a certain shrill shout has become almost common. But this sound was different — *older*. Not like the sound the baby stars make when they are grabbed from behind by the terrorists, not like the sound the baby stars make when their film deals fall through, not like the sound of squirming pain the baby stars make when their series are cancelled — but *older*. Sally Molloy guided me toward the sound. The sound had been made by Willy Hoem, of course. We saw him in his room. Attached to the most expensive life-support devices, kept alive at outrageous expense in a room contrived to resemble the more simple medical facility where you first saw him, that great man continued to scream. Then suddenly he fell quiet. I turned around and Sally Molloy was gone. I kept still. Willy made a further noise. I wondered if he was trying to sing — to sing "Me and Misericordia," for instance, which was such a great influence on you, or "Rooming," or "No Land, None," those great songs of work and effort. I unhooked the velvet rope in front of Willy's bed and moved closer. It was very hard to find a musical reference point for the sounds Willy was making.

Then I went from room to room without guidance. There were rooms for each of your albums, rooms for each of your women. Some of your women were in their rooms. The rooms for the more important women had signs in log frames listing the references to them in your songs if your songs referred to them, listing other pertinent information if their significance to you was extramusical. I found Sally Molloy in her room, with two signs — one musical in thrust, the other general. The room was like a room in one of the big hotels from the days of rage, when you stood with Sally and Forman Jurl and Willy Hoem outside the big hotels — all dressed in velvet, with *that smile* on your face, just that wreath of insight on your lips — waiting for the police to bring their big thumbs through your eyes. I noticed a pinball machine in the room — not a "Recent Scores," which is the machine you license now, but a "Keep Clear," one of the old ones you have had withdrawn from circulation, carted away, and destroyed. "Keep

Clear" was the anthem of a generation, and the "Keep Clear" machine was the machine of the days of rage — the first machine you authorized to be manufactured in your name. This one was in bad repair, but I could see the terrific quality: the double thickness of rubber on the flippers, the vivid colors on the game board, the extra features, like the Bonus Whirl. I tried to play the "Keep Clear," but it tilted right away. I tried to stand next to Sally Molloy, but I saw that it didn't mean a thing.

"This room is an accurate replica of one of the rooms in one of the big hotels," Sally said mechanically. "It may interest you to know that it was in a room just like this that Sammy told me to leave, told me we couldn't stay together, told me I couldn't stay with him, told me that I didn't have any talent, not really. I was a singer myself, you know, and a poet," Sally said.

A: Is that as far as you've gotten?

Q: Well, *almost* as far as I've gotten.

A: And you're a little nervous now?

Q: No! Not nervous!

A: So you wouldn't mind if we got to the *film?* If we began to talk about the *film?*

Q: Your film is about identity, of course. That shifting of masks. When you sing "Token Bitch" as Elia onstage. In the mask. When you whisper, over and over, "Beyond that!" When you enter that sharp intersection between questions of personal identity, which the songs bring up literally, and questions of who we were then, which your very presence brings up.

A: But perhaps it seemed insufficiently filmic? A little self-indulgent?

Q: When you appear as Lamb, we can see that the tension between intersection and juxtaposition is the generational force that produced the songs — the songs that, of course, we already know:

The shoes
Stiff with lies,
I turned in
with my old friend, my old friend.

The songs that we had seen as intersection between you and us but had yet to see as juxtaposition between you and you.

A: Is that what you get out of it?

Q: Well, not all I get out of it.

A: I wonder if you could tell me what else. It's the most natural thing in the world not to get the point the first few times.

Q: The girl waiting through the dawn, outside the big hotel, with a piece of velvet. The motion away from the cheap materials, like I grew up with. Away from the ready-made, which was all there was at one point.

A: Could you tell me what else?

Q: The pleasure of being with you. Your birth and growth and so on. "Just like your/Justice" is about being born, of course. "I can't keep you . . . guilty/Or not" — your big head being born.

A: Did you by any remote chance hear me say "Twin vision, twin vision, twin vision/Twin vision, twin vision, twin vision, twin vision"?

Q: Certan rabbis feel that there are four kinds of vision. Single vision, as when Elia sings "Mangled Me" in the lobby. The vision of the double and the self, as when Elia and Lamb appear together. The vision of the triple sense, which I forget just how it goes. And then the fourth vision — the double doubled — as in "twin vision."

A: I don't feel that you've gone very deep. Do you feel you have?

Q: Sometimes I stop short. Sometimes I leave a small portion for you. For the extra power in you.

A: All that is in the promotional literature. Have you had time to examine the promotional literature?

Q: Well, no. We've been watching the film pretty steadily.

A: Too much? Have we spent too much time watching the film?

Q: Oh, no!

A: You don't think it's too long? Some of the distributors have said it's too long. They said there is a big problem and I might have to four-wall it. Take it to stupid little towns, one by one. Repellent. I planned the most beautiful film. I planned the most beautiful promotional literature. Total color. Four-color promotional literature. Every nuance of red. You saw what they gave me. You call that a beautiful red?

Q: I was a nothing. Just a nobody. In a state school. Nasty glazed brick. Those small-paned windows set too high up in the wall. I had a nobody for a girlfriend. That stringy hair you can't do anything with. Oh, you can wash it, all right, but it never has any fullness or shine.

A: This big room. I wonder if it isn't too metallic. I wonder if there isn't going to be an emphasis on fabric I ought to pick up on. Are you sure you're comfortable here?

Q: It's a little tight. Maybe a little too tight. Maybe I shouldn't be this rigid. What are you doing?

A: I'm going to run it again.

Obstruction

I STEP INTO the elevator. It is an old elevator. One of the great old elevators. Bands of aggressive metal binding in pastels. The ascent is not quite smooth, but then in *those days* there was no emphasis on ascent itself — the novelty was enough. And the decoration. That incredible care. Smooth bands of chrome turning the corners (smoothing the angles into curves), providing just that *frisson* of claustrophobia sufficient to draw one's mind to the experience. None of that now, of course. None of that care. No understanding of the heavy colors. And all the trash asked to all the parties.

The elevator stops. By pulling apart the doors with all my force, I can see a reception area. The doors fly open. A receptionist is startled. She fingers her throat. She is wearing one of the new medic-alert necklaces. It spells out "Diabetes" in electroplate script. She recognizes me and smiles.

I enter the office of Morgan Aspair, the daughter of the legendary producer Hemming Aspair and herself a film entrepreneur. I just slip in and sit in the corner and don't say a word. Sometimes when I interview people, I go to the door and ring the bell and take out my pad and sit in an obvious chair and ask questions like "In trying to reach an opinion about the word 'feminine' versus the word 'feminist,' is there any contradiction in the fact that in your last film you play a very feminine woman — in the sense that she gives up her job in Legal Aid to go travelling around the country looking for a man — while in your personal life you continue to be identified with radical feminist causes?" Sometimes I do more in-depth work. On the tape recorder. Staying close to get the atmosphere, going through the open drawers, looking through the stubs.

Morgan, at this moment, is having trouble catching her breath. The feeling, I know, is of a small obstruction. Small in that she cannot be sure exactly where it is. Small in that she may be imagining it. She uses short, rapid intakes of breath. Into a rhythm, and then the obstruction (or the *sense* of the obstruction) lessens. Her left hand goes to her throat to feel the pulse there, and the rhythm of breathing. The charm bracelet on her left wrist makes small noises. I know that bracelet, from many days of slipping into this office and watching. Different charms from different times. A tiny gold cocktail shaker. A mustard seed encased in crystal. A replica of her father's house at the beach, done to scale. "The good times, the big times — the times with a gloss on them," as Morgan has said. Morgan takes one charm between the thumb and forefinger of her right hand: a tiny gold woman and tiny gold man. Morgan says, as though to herself, "Look. The woman has rolled stock-ings. The man has anklets. Who would have the fineness to understand that now? The subtlety?" She pauses. Possibly so that I can catch up.

Morgan drops the charm and brings the index finger of her right hand to the telephone on her desk. The telephone dial makes little *skew* sounds under the pressure of her finger. It is a familiar pattern of sounds — evidence of a call to Vanessa, her sister, in New York. Morgan holds the receiver in the air — perhaps so I can hear. Vanessa's phone rings and rings.

I put my right hand into the right front pocket of my trousers. Making almost no sound, I touch a newspaper clipping I have placed there. With only a slight rustle, I bring the clipping from my pocket. It is a clipping from the "Billy Whisper" column:

"*Vanessa Aspair* sits by her phone, lets it ring and ring, *just won't take her sister's calls.* Billy Whisper didn't want to tell. . . . Billy Whisper tried to keep it quiet. . . . Billy Whisper *couldn't like it more.*"

Then Morgan says, "Billy Whisper is such a vicious, vicious liar. Billy Whisper is such filthy, filthy scum. I could see Billy Whisper with his teeth pushed down his throat." I replace the clipping in my pocket. Immediately Morgan is less tense, experiences less stress. Our communication is that close. "Columnists used to have such style," she says. "All my little birthday parties. All the people who came. In the columns, *always.*" I notice a little hesitation in Morgan's voice. This means that she wants to know if I am in the mood to have her talk about all the old columns, all those great old items. I keep a certain silence, and Morgan senses that we should talk less about the great old columns and more about Vanessa just at this moment.

She takes a little pause, time enough for a small shift in emphasis, time enough to evade the obstruction in her throat. Then she says, "Vanessa was in the columns, naturally. But *less often*. Mentioned in the *lists*. Filling out the room. Coming in later. It wasn't her fault, of course. At least, not at first. But she *was* stingy in her affections — Daddy thought so, too — and resentful. Because I won the Dream Search when I was fourteen. Because I had blond hair falling straight down my back. Because I said 'You and what army?' to Jimmy Cagney in such a cute way when I was six that he gave me a whole little army of marzipan soldiers — which were *lead*, actually, with a thin layer of marzipan over the metal, *which I knew*, but which came as a surprise to Vanessa when she *stole* them and *bit into them* and ended up in a situation where she had to have a lot of work done in her mouth. Resentful. And hurt because I was so close to Daddy. Always so close to Daddy."

Morgan turns back to the work on her desk. There are some scripts on her desk, and three manila folders. She works with the scripts, arranging them in a way I understand. All at once she takes a piece of paper from one of the folders and places it *on top of* the folder. Sometimes when Morgan does this, it means that she wants me to look at the piece of paper involved if I can do it without her catching me. I move forward in my chair. After a few moments, I stand up. I take one step. I can read the word "Daddy" on the folder tab. I take two steps. I can read every word on the paper. It is a letter from Alice Rice:

> Your father was a terribly attractive man. Terribly attractive to women. If he spilled wine on your dress, or pinched you till you bruised, or did anything difficult, he sent flowers the next day, *always*. He was a gentleman. One is shy about saying that nowadays, but that was the truth of it. I remember once at my house (it was Bel Air, I think, before we moved to the beach — I don't know where you were, but not there — maybe away at school?) I was a little upset. I was upset, frankly, because I'd lost the lead in *Designing Woman* to Betty Bacall, who was fabulous in the part and who had a name that rhymed in the way the *promotion people* wanted — I don't know if you remember the slogan but it was "Peck and Bacall, and That's Not All!" — and, of course, now I'm thrilled that she got to play it, but *then*, to be honest, I was a little upset. And your father just looked at me — that *look* of his, all those disfigurements momentarily effaced — and he looked straight at me — I remember it perfectly — and he said, "Shit, Mouse, I'll get you the part." That tough-guy voice, you see. Hiding the real manners. Very attractive. Of course, he never did a thing about it. Not even a phone call. But the *gesture*, you see. And, of course, he adored you. All

those lots on Melrose Avenue he gave you. And the airplane hangar, or *what was that?*

Morgan twists her body to the right, away from me, using her left elbow as a pivot. Then she slides her elbow and lower arm very slightly in my direction. Morgan has moved another letter toward me, *as though by accident.* Once the letter is within my view, Morgan lifts her arm and turns her back. The letter is from Jimmy Boam:

> Your father was a very charming person despite some problems. Your father was terrified, certainly, but he had great style. I remember once when he was coming back from Honolulu (this was before he became so terrified of travel) and we were together on one of those big Matson Line steamers that used to have so much style, and he began to cry and cry and cry in the little ship's library (which was done in blond veneer, the kind we used to think was so attractive! — which I threw out of the Brentwood house, finally, six or seven years ago, the blond veneer stuff that I had, just before it came back in style!) and I thought, Here we go again, but he pulled himself together in time for drinks. That was just before I did *Mr. Smith Goes to Washington* with Jimmy Stewart.

Morgan turns around in her seat. She faces me directly, which is rarely done under the terms of our special arrangement. "We had it all," she says violently. "All that *style*."

As she turns away, I notice a crumpled piece of paper on the floor. I pick it up. Taking infinite pains, I open it, smoothing one wrinkle at a time, doing the loud parts during those moments when Morgan herself has made a noise. It is the last page of a handwritten letter. At the top of the page there is a simple engraved line: "From the Desk of Mr. Romino." Underneath this there is a vivacious logo, reading "Paul Romino's Vine Room." I know that logo — of course I do. It spread all over the Vine Room: on those giant menus, on the individual signs at each table, which were meant to be stolen and the cost of which was figured into the cover charge, which was stiff. I read the writing on the page:

> Later, perhaps, not so good. But you remember the birthday party — was it perhaps for *you*? In *your* honor? When he put your head in the cake and held it down until the Turkish men who kept the towels in the bathroom grabbed his arms and pinned them behind his back? Was this, perhaps, about the time *So Glad* was such a large success? That amusing show about competition among resorts?

Morgan leaves the building. I follow at a distance. On the street, I see her in her new Buick, parked at the curb. I take a newspaper from a dispensing machine at the corner and move casually down the street past Morgan's Buick. I notice that the rear door on the curb side has been left unlocked. I open the door and enter the car. The car pulls into traffic. Morgan drives with great energy and distinction. She slips an eight-track tape into the machine. For a few moments there is music: snippets of "If You Need Me," by Wilson Pickett, and "Funny," by Maxine Brown, for instance. Making as little noise as possible, I open the newspaper to the "Billy Whisper" column. The third item says:

"*Vanessa Aspair* won't pick up her sister's calls, and will make her own deal at Paramount, taking her mastectomy script with her. Billy Whisper ought to keep it quiet. . . . Billy Whisper ought to look the other way. . . . But Billy Whisper *couldn't like it more.*"

Morgan has the sense of a small obstruction in her throat. She puts her left hand to the top of her throat and tries to establish a rhythm of breathing. Then she brings her left hand down to the steering wheel, and with the index finger of her right hand she changes the program on the tape. I hear her voice on the new program — something she has recorded. At the same time, I hear the small gasps she makes, live, as she seeks to establish a helpful rhythm of breathing. On the tape, the voice of Morgan says, "*That day.*" There is a pause. I sit silently in my seat. We drive past Costello's, which was the first drive-in restaurant on Wilshire Boulevard. In that great nineteen-fifties style.

"*That day*," Morgan's voice says again on the tape. "Daddy picked me up at school, in the Buick. 'Up for a spin, Doll?' was the way he put it. Jaunty, always.

"The Buick was a Roadmaster convertible, with four portholes on the side. Daddy pointed to the portholes. Daddy said, 'Did you ever notice that when you buy the cheapest Buick, you get only three? Did you notice that when you move up to the next class, you get only three? And in the next class, still only three? *You got to go all the way to the top of the line to get that fourth porthole, Doll.*'

"*That day*. We stopped at a roadside restaurant, Daddy and I. Inside, it was all red. Red checked oilcloth had been glued to the hatch doors where the different flavors of ice cream were kept. Beverages were served in big tumblers of red glass. We sat in a booth. What did we talk about that day? Daddy had a million plans. *Rendez-Vous* was a smash hit, and he wanted to take it on tour — not with Minnah Murray, who was the star, but with Alice Rice. He wanted Minnah to stay in New York and go into rehearsal with *Gale Force Winds*, a calypso musical. On the personal side there were some problems. I think we talked about my brother, Mike, who had run away from the Sledge School to join Castro in Cuba but who had had an attack of poor nerves in Florida and was resting in Orlando. I think we talked about Mother, who had been arrested for 'lawning' — driving her powerful Chevrolet station wagon deep into the newly planted lawns of twenty or thirty suburban homes. Daddy was full of energy and wit and affection. What Vanessa has called 'the magic of Daddy.'

"Unfortunately, I got carried away and brought up the troublesome issue of spending Christmas and New Year's at home instead of under supervision. Daddy just looked at me. 'You know that's my pet peeve, Doll — all that stuff,' he said. I smiled and slipped one of the big red tumblers into my lap."

Morgan changes the program on the tape:

"*Mother*. Mother in red. Mother whipping the red checked cloth off the table in the Bel Air 'Play House' to play like a bandit. Just her eyes peeking over the cloth. Flashing eyes — like a bandit. No one could amuse like Mother. But forgetful, sometimes. Tying Mike up and putting him in the sports closet (where there was every kind of thing — the big croquet mallets from England, those wickets made from the good heavy wire, the *good* birdies for badminton) and leaving him there for the weekend when she meant it to be just until the end of a screening. And *aggressive*. When she walked into the tack room and saw Daddy with Lilly Landa, when she saw that Daddy had his tongue in Lilly Landa's ear, she killed the dogs. Twelve of them. Those cocker spaniels people used to have. Beautiful. But high-strung. So different from the Mother the public knew in *Pleasure Craft* and *Signal Me* and *The Roentgen Story*."

This is new material. Morgan has held my interest. She turns off the machine so I can catch up.

* * *

The car stops for a traffic light. I notice a man in a vulgar car. After the light changes, the vulgar car keeps pace with our Buick. Morgan looks straight ahead. I look straight ahead. Then the vulgar car *squeezes left* so that we are forced to stop. I look straight ahead. However, I sense that the man has approached our car. "May I see your license and registration?" the man asks. Morgan looks over at him. I look over. I see that the man is Johnny Taffe, new head of production at Universal, where Morgan was going to have her own deal. Quickly, I turn away and look straight ahead. Morgan continues to look at Johnny Taffe. He has tricked her. In terms of body movement and eye contact, and in terms of modifying another person's response to conform with one's expectations and interests, he has won. At the moment of his maximum energy output he throws three scripts through the front window of the Buick on the passenger side.

"Sorry, sweetie, I have to pass on these," he says. "The one in the green cover didn't have a hook; the one in the red cover didn't have a part; the one in the brown cover just didn't get me off." He goes back to his car and calls over his shoulder, "Not that I have to give my reasons."

Sometimes when Morgan is a little upset, she drives past her lots. Morgan owns land on Melrose Avenue. She drives past her lots now. She toots her horn as we go by. Then she stops the car, gets out, and goes to a telephone booth. Out of respect for her privacy I stay in the car.

Morgan has turned the eight-track tape machine back on, out of consideration for me. But it is an old program. One I know by heart. About the columns. About the winter of 1955, when Hemming Aspair took her off sedation. Took her out on the town for two months and then dropped her cold. "That blond Hemming Aspair took nightclubbing — to the Blue Boat, to the Big Ball Club, to Jamey Torey Fortune's — was *me*," Morgan's voice says. "Morgan, just ten, took his calls, sipped from his drink, checked his new gray hat."

Reaching over the front seat, I hit the program button and interrupt Morgan's voice. Sometimes when Morgan begins to talk *too much* (live or on tape) — about the old night clubs, the columns, and so forth — I get a little edgy and we have to switch topics.

The topic on the new program has to do with real estate, which suits my mood better. "Daddy gave me different kinds of property for tax reasons sometimes," Morgan's voice says on the tape. "Mary Ann, Daddy's secretary, would call and say could I sign some papers, and I'd go into the office, and Mary Ann would say, 'Here and here and here,' and I'd sign. Then she'd tell me what it was. I got the lots on Melrose that way, and an antique shop, and a percentage of *Pleasure Craft*, and part ownership of an airplane hangar. One time I tried to take a few friends from my Attention Group to see the airplane hangar, but we couldn't find it, so I took them by the lots on Melrose Avenue instead. That was a bad time, because it frightened Daddy when I mentioned it and he wouldn't speak to me for several months. Some years later, over drinks, he explained that the airplane hangar was more of an airplane hangar *on paper* than it was an actual building. I said I was sorry that I had done something to frighten him, but that just made him angry."

I watch Morgan in the telephone booth. I can tell that the sense of obstruction has become more powerful. Her mouth is open, but her lips do not move. My reading of her total physical stance is that she is gasping, not having a telephone conversation. When she returns to the car, she is shaking very slightly. She takes the car into traffic and with her right index finger changes the program on the tape machine.

"*That day,*" says her voice on tape. "That day, in the roadside restaurant, Daddy got very excited and made promise after promise. He promised me a spot on 'Wisecrack Alley'—a popular television show during the nineteen-fifties, where precocious children tried to 'top' professional entertainers. He promised to let me wear more suggestive clothing. I was very happy. The waitress saw that we were having a good time and said that we looked nice together. The afternoon sun was coming in through the windows, which had red curtains. Two very fat people were sitting together, laughing and laughing. I looked at them. Daddy said something I didn't hear, and I said, 'What?' Then Daddy got angry and said the whole day was spoiled. I said I was very sorry. When I said that, Daddy got mad. Daddy was silent almost all the way back to where I was being held under supervision. The only thing he said was 'You can forget about "Wisecrack Alley," Doll, embarrassing me that way in front of strangers.' "

Morgan changes the program on the tape. The next program is Bad Charley singing "Turn to the Ladies." Morgan turns off the tape machine. She looks at me in the rear-view mirror. Eye contact is unusual under the terms of our special arrangement.

"I called Vanessa," Morgan says. "She didn't pick up. I called her service, and they said she's at home but isn't picking up. Then I called my service, and they said that Vanessa left a message not to bother to call, because she has her own deal at Paramount."

Morgan lowers her eyes and turns the tape machine back on. She drives with great intensity.

"*Daddy,*" Morgan's voice says on the tape. "The night he told me that he and Mother were getting a divorce, he pulled out a pistol. He aimed right at me and pulled the trigger, but all it did was go *click*. 'Just another misfire, Doll,' Daddy said."

We head toward Pasadena. Sometimes when Morgan is very upset, she takes us to Pasadena to see "Dolly" Madison, her father's best friend and for years the top gossip columnist in the country — not just for the Hollywood trash but for the real social crowd. Dolly comes from a very fine family and grew up in a famous house on the North Shore of Long Island, but when the zoning was overthrown, he moved West. He gave up his daily column when he moved, but he continues to write a monthly roundup for *SnoWest Leisure,* a very influential magazine distributed free at ski resorts. In some ways, Morgan is closer to Dolly Madison than to anyone else, maybe because he seems to belong to another world — her father's world, where style and class counted for something.

The tires of our Buick make a noise on the bluestone of Dolly's driveway. Dolly has the *good* bluestone, and the noise is luxurious. The door is opened by an impeccable Irish maid in a starched uniform trimmed with lace. I look just below her lace collar (because I know to look there), and I see the tiny legend "Property of Universal Players." It is Dolly's whim that his servants should come from cancelled television series. He pays close attention to the ratings and hovers around marginal shows in a way that producers find unnerving.

The maid shows us to the patio, where Dolly is sitting in a little wrought-iron chair in front of a wrought-iron table, upon which tea things have been laid. Dolly is the last person in Los Angeles to have tea every afternoon. On the table there is an arrangement of the most delicious-looking cakes and cookies. Pastries stuffed with the richest cream and chocolate, tiny shells filled with fresh, fresh berries, and scones made with the finest ingredients. This is terribly generous of Dolly, because he can't keep a thing down, himself, and lives on artificial nutrients.

"Now, darling, I want *all* your news," Dolly says, his small hand on Morgan's sleeve. Morgan does not bring up Vanessa's deal with Paramount. She tells him about one or two problems her daughter, Clarke, thirteen, is having keeping her hands to herself, and about a project that is very important to her — a remake of *Rampant*, her father's picture about alcoholism in the legal profession, updated to encompass drug abuse.

"But, of course, *Rampant* was not a success," Dolly says. "I mean, when your father did it. Have one of those delicious little chocolate cakes."

Morgan takes a chocolate cake and explains that she wants to remake *Rampant* as a *tribute* to her father.

"Now, *that's* sweet," Dolly says. He looks closely at her chocolate cake. "Maybe I'll just have a small bite," he says.

"What went wrong, Dolly?" Morgan asks suddenly. "We had everything."

"Wrong?" Dolly says. "Nothing went wrong. You *still* have everything." He makes a small sound and removes the bite of cake from his mouth. "The truth of it is," he says, "I can't keep a thing down."

Do You Know Me?

I WAS WELL KNOWN. I was so well known everyone knew me. I was the best-known person in the world. I put on my plaid shirt and my thick boots and the thin-wale corduroy pants and I was the best-known person in the world. And then I went slowly. I looked in the mirror. I wore the thin-wale corduroy pants because I think the thick-wale is effeminate. I went out my door. I went down the stairs. I lived on the second floor — no indoor entrance; I had to walk up and down outside stairs to get in and out. Outside stairs. My outside stairs. My weather-stained porch. Not a very pretty porch. No room for a nice chair. Paint peeling off, just like loneliness sloughing off the skin. Onto the sidewalk. I walked onto the sidewalk, watched the sidewalk, focused on the sidewalk. I saw my thick boots only as a blur. So cracked, that sidewalk. The little shoots of grass, the roots of trees working the cement into dust. I was so well known that that sidewalk was well known.

I was quite well known when I was still quite young. I had many friends. Bobbi and Sammi and Tadi and Ronee and Bilye. I had so many friends. I liked friends who were girls but had boys' names, but ending in a different letter than a boy's name would. That was the kind of friend I wanted, and that was the kind of friend I had. That was my preference. My preference was for people just like that. I wanted to be specific. I wanted to be so specific that no one would have any doubts. That was the only reason I was that well known. Because it was so specific. Because there wasn't any doubt. People with a name like Sammi or Ronee or Jami or Tonee knew that kind of name was my preference. That made me well known.

Would you know me if I showed you my papers? Would you know me if I showed you my Bulldog Editions? Would you know me if I showed you my Special Home Editions? Would you let me show you the Blue Final and the Final Blue? Will you glance at my papers? Will you have a look? Do you know me when you have a look? Do you know me when I call you on the phone? Do you know me when I walk on the sidewalk, when I watch the cracks? Do you lie there and think, "It's him. He's on the sidewalk"?

Do you remember the texture of my nose? The slightly grainy texture, as though it had been rubbed and rubbed and rubbed? Do you have a general impression of my face — just that, a *general* impression? Nothing more than that? Just a vague feeling that the face is a type of face, a face of a type that a certain kind of person would have? Is it *abstract*, the way you feel, when I tried so hard to supply detail? I wanted everything so clear, so specific. I went to so much trouble. I dressed in a certain way. I dressed three times. I put on my clothes and then I took them off, and then I put them on and then I took them off, and then I put them on in a final way that was very specific. Then I walked slowly. Keeping my eye on the pavement. I made the pavement so specific. I made my friends so specific. Sometimes it happened that they thought they were general, but they were wrong. I made them specific, down to the details. I knew all the details and went over them three times. That was my preference.

Do you remember my preference? Do you remember the way I made them nervous? That was part of the preference. Do you remember the way I made them reluctant to wear their uniforms in public? That was part of my preference. So specific, my preference. So specific, the way the little uniforms looked under a big bulky coat. Would you know me if I wore a uniform? Would you know me if I wore a bulky coat? Would you know me if I moved a step closer? Would you know me if I took off my hat? Would you know me if I showed you a clipping? Would you know me if I took a clipping and circled my name so it would stand out, and then attached a small piece of white paper (with gum or mucilage) with my name typed out just like my name typed out on the Linotypes and on the wire services and on the special identification cards they require in so many places, typed out on plastic? Would you know me if I typed my name out? Would you know me if I asked you for a dime? Would you know me if I asked to walk you home?

Bullies

"THAT WAS my frontier," the old man said, raising his hand, unfolding it, looking at it, then looking at it more closely, as if to note the absence of a proper tool. "That was my frontier. None of the grain or the hills or the wide-open space. It was the laying out of the streets. That was my frontier. I remember when the streets were laid out."

Mr. Sal Margineaux put his foot closer to his chair. He put his mind somewhere else. That was his gift. That was part of his gift. He put his foot on the floor and touched the heel of his foot to the plinth of his chair. He put his mind somewhere else. It was the ambition of Sal Margineaux (and very often his achievement) to be well grounded, to be well grounded secretly (touching both the ground, perhaps, and a chair, perhaps, in a way that wasn't observed) — to do this and then to put his mind somewhere else. The old man continued to talk, but it didn't mean a thing.

"I remember when they put through Arthur. Arthur Boulevard," the old man said. "We didn't know it would be so wide. For a while, that's all there was, just Arthur, very wide, and then they cut across, not disorderly but like they knew the pattern. Upland Hover, that was a nice street. And Frangen. Frangen ran in a line with Arthur, of course, but not so wide. Upland Hover and Frangen was a nice corner. Years ago, when they put it through — years ago, when they put it through but didn't build — years ago, you could stand at the corner of Upland Hover and Frangen and see five of the stations. Four were up. One was rising. You could see the Gerland Street Station rising."

For a while, the old man stood silently, which Sal Margineaux noticed but didn't mind, because he had put his mind somewhere else, and then the old man left and Sal Margineaux called out to a woman who worked for him, a woman who touched his hands just where he said to, who kept a certain kind of blouse on, a blouse like a man's shirt but not a man's shirt, a blouse just like a shirt of silk but not silk — he called out to this woman and said, "I don't want to see any more of these old men."

The old man walked out from Mr. Sal Margineaux's office, past a series of works of art. Various shades of red, the old man thought. Then his mind returned to the things he did think about when nothing was drawn especially into it. He thought about his daughter and about his neatness of person, about his abstinence from liquor, and about the proper maintenance of his tools and equipment. He saw the woman who worked for Mr. Margineaux as she walked past, because she seemed like something in a film — not only because she was dressed in the vivid way he associated with people in films but because of the long, empty quality of her walking down the hall.

The woman didn't notice him. Boop-boop-a-doop. Down the hall, swinging her hips, shaking them through the skirt. The skirt was pulled that tight. A man's belt cinched it in. Boop-boop-a-doop. She said to herself, "Don't mess with me. Mess with me. Please mess with me. Take your thumb and outline the nipple on my breast. Do it. Do it. Too tough to do it? Not tough enough. Show me a grin. Show me a smile. Take my place?" Later, she thought, I'm reading. I'm a girl who reads. In fact, she was a girl who liked to read. She was reading the story of Emma Ford, a big dark woman who broke the necks of men. A Negro woman who wore a hat. Didn't smile. Wore a hat and knew the judge. "Fine me, I got money" was Emma Ford's point of view. Later, the woman thought, I live in the city. I'm a girl who lives in town. She came from a small city. Where she grew up, there was a street with a big old theatre and a big old courthouse. And a store. More than one store, but one store that seemed right. It seemed to belong to the idea of the city. "Maregll Shops," it said, in a kind of script. It wasn't a branch store. It wasn't the little arm of something bigger. That would have been depressing to her. It was full-size, in its way. No other town had a bigger one. But there were others. That was nice. Other

Maregll Shops in other places. Full-size. That was nice. The theatre and the courthouse and the Maregll Shops shop were full-size. "Everything else was just nothing," she said when she thought of it.

Mr. Sal Margineaux found that his attention had turned to the old man. He sat still and waited for this to change. "Margineaux Corporation Was Going Great Guns" — he kept his mind on that. His lips moved. "Margineaux Corporation Was Going Great Guns" — he moved his lips over that. "Then . . ." He stopped. "Then . . ." He stopped. "Margineaux Corporation Was Going Great Guns" — he kept his mind on that. He thought he might ask the girl to touch him on the hand. She might challenge him. That got his attention. She might try to slip under him or away from him or into a place he kept safe. That would be interesting. He hired her because she was interested in criminal women. He felt safe with a person like that.

Mr. Frank Margineaux was another story. Mr. Sal Margineaux looked after the financial side — took the papers, kept the papers, laid the papers out, sifted the papers into sense, and shot the papers at people in a way that made them sit down. Small and thin, with a tiny nose, wearing glasses graded in color from dark to light and wearing shoes with trim in real brass and carrying a brown leather envelope, Sal Margineaux handled the rapid movements of the Margineaux Corporation, which were aggressive, often. Frank Margineaux was another story. Frank Margineaux had a weakness just under the skin. Sometimes he had to buy a car or join a health club or make a woman absorb his fear. His gift was that he knew how to make people embarrassed and alarmed, using his weakness. He kept to the company of people who preferred to be hit rather than be embarrassed or alarmed. Thus he was protected, in a way. But he didn't believe in protection, not any that worked for more than a minute, so he was on edge a lot, and was unable to maintain anything, and had to have things that were new: new women, new clothes, and so forth. He was not able to trust anyone; least of all was he able to trust Sal Margineaux or to trust his own success. Frank Margineaux was in the construction side. He gave parties.

At about the time that the displaced old men began to assemble in new places and to consult with lawyers and to request interviews with Mr. Sal Margineaux—at about that time, Mr. Frank Margineaux met a girl at one of his boat-club parties who looked him up and down and drew the weakness to the surface and kept it there and did not become embarrassed or alarmed. That may have been the beginning of the problem. This girl began to service Frank Margineaux. That may have been the beginning of the problem. She did anything he said, but when she got up she smoothed her dress as though she had just finished a minor errand in the kitchen and was thinking about going out to a movie, and when she looked at him she was unembarrassed and unalarmed, and he was unsmoothed and still wrinkled, and sometimes dirty and sometimes wet. That may have been the beginning of the problem.

Until the time when the old men began to assemble in unexpected places, until the time when Mr. Frank Margineaux began to undergo severe stress, spending days and days wrinkled and not clean, and then ripping things away from him, and then crying and crying and then buying in gluts, buying stores and warehouses and not keeping track of what he bought, and putting new things on and then ripping them off right away — until that time, Margineaux Corporation was going great guns. The business in outfitting special spaces — laying down the special mats impregnated with a special antiseptic but in a secret way so the antiseptic couldn't eat through, corrode the surface, flake off into the air, and lodge in the lungs — that business was going great guns. The business in abandoned spaces — that business was going great guns. Frank Margineaux did the construction and Sal Margineaux had a certain way. He handled papers in a way that brought power to the surface of his desk. From where? From ancient pens, rotting now, from ancient pens where thirty thousand animals in a short time came and stayed and were slaughtered; from the system of chutes and the system of hooks on a chain and the deep cellars, where special use was found for entrails and blood and snouts and the lids of pigs' eyes, where everything was efficient at first (this was long ago) and then old and then insecure. Power came to Sal Margineaux from every place where energy, abundant in the deepest ways, had ceased to rise to the surface. Sal Margineaux knew the value of a surface. He knew how to tease a surface and bring the energy up again, how to make it rise like something out of sleep, something rising up angry out of sleep. He was the first to understand abandoned spaces. He was the first to understand small cities, for instance, where there was just nothing —a courthouse, a theatre, a line of boardinghouses full of dangerous people. He was the first to understand old buildings with great rooms where people wouldn't go. He understood concourses and rotundas, and he understood packinghouses and the districts around packinghouses, and warehouses and commercial developments and terminals, and the use of terminals in the context of loneliness, and the use of space in the context of fear, and he understood paper.

Scratch. Scratch. Scratch. The old man walked away from the offices of Margineaux Corporation. He stopped for a cup of tea. He sat at a counter, a nice marble counter kept clean. He looked at his shoes. Nicely polished. He drank his tea. He left. After he had walked for a long time, a friend fell in beside him. The friend talked and continued to talk. The old man didn't listen. At the end of what he was saying, the friend said, "Years ago."

"Years ago," the old man said.

They walked together, keeping clear of the mud. No mud got on their shoes. They came to Van Rayn Street, which was at the edge of the district where they used to stand. Van Rayn Street had been on the edge before. At first, it had been on the edge of how far in that direction a nice person would live, and then on the edge of how far in that direction a nice person would look for pleasure, and now on the edge in the sense that it continued to exist while just over the edge there was nothing — only streets heaving up, block after block reverting to rubble and then to land and then to something less than land, something eked out with a certain kind of special matting, sprayed with a certain kind of disinfectant, marked off by a certain kind of fence. The old man stood on Van Rayn Street with his friend. There were old men up and down Van Rayn Street. Some old men were neat. They wore cardigan sweaters over neat gray shirts with the top button buttoned. Some old men were very neat and had polished shoes. Some old men carried a tool or wore a holder for a tool. These men had worked for the Shield Fresh Company and the Framod Packing Corporation and the Great Six Railroads and the Rapic Terminals and the Georgic Refrigerated Car Company and the Pale Rolling Stock Company and the Youreng Mechanical Farmer Corporation. They had known old Mr. Ponor, who had lived for so long, and old Mr. Framod and Mr. Jandon and the Rapic brothers. They stood on Van Rayn Street, but it was depressing just to stand and look at the old streets heaving up, so after a little while most of them went to stand in one of the theatres on Van Rayn Street — in the Brabant or the Luxor-Karnak or the Frame or the Rhinelander Photoplay.

The old man and his friend went to the Rhinelander Photoplay. They stood at the back. Many other old men stood at the back, watching the screen as though they were looking down a dark road. They could make out some things, but they didn't say a word. They stood close together, but they didn't say a word. They made their space into a pattern and stood at the corners. The films they watched, like other films shown on Van Rayn Street, were a combination of poor sex and interviewing. The men stood impassively, as if this was what they expected from a film. Some of the films seemed to take place in England but referred to the way things were done in America. Some of these films had plots that showed different people having the upper hand at different moments. A man would arrive in an expensive car, for instance, and it looked as if he would have the upper hand. Then he would be greeted by a pretty woman, who would kiss him and say "Umm" afterward, so it still looked as if he had the upper hand. But then she might lead him somewhere specific, so it was in doubt that he had the upper hand, and she might make him wear something specific or do something specific, so it was in doubt, and then she might say something like, "Ummmm, no, not this way. Let's go to the greenhouse," and then at the greenhouse there would be another man. It was very tentative sometimes. But it seemed to be just what the old men expected in a film. Sometimes it was boring, though, and the old men coughed a little. Sometimes the arrival scenes went on too long.

WOMAN: Hello. You're a little late.
MAN: This is quite a place you have here.
WOMAN: Here, I'll show you where to take your things.

Sometimes when the arrival scenes went on too long or there were long shots of the house or there was too much awkward dancing — sometimes then the old men coughed and talked softly to one another.

Mr. Frank Margineaux and his girlfriend:

GIRLFRIEND: Here, let me wipe you off.
FRANK: I don't need to wipe anything off.
GIRLFRIEND: Why don't you *tell* me to wipe you off?
FRANK: Wipe it off!
GIRLFRIEND: Mmmmm.
FRANK: That's it! Wipe it off!
GIRLFRIEND: Mmmmmmmm.
FRANK: Yeah. Yeah.
GIRLFRIEND: You look so tired. I've never seen you tired. Are you tired? Are you too tired? Do you want to sit down? I wonder why you get so tired. I wonder what's on. There you are — so tired! Here you are —

so wrinkled! What do you do to get so dirty? That's what I wonder. What's on, I wonder. I hope it isn't just the news.

Mr. Sal Margineaux left his office and walked to the boat-club party given by Mr. Frank Margineaux. Frank Margineaux gave a boat-club party almost every night. Frank Margineaux had bought up the names and the artifacts of nine boat clubs. He left the piers rotting in the lake, fenced off the property, moved the boat clubs to different secure suites in office buildings, and gave parties at them almost every night. There were so many nice artifacts! Lacquered oars crossed on the wall, tied with black leather thongs, the blades curving nicely outward; silver urns, elaborate in their decoration — challenge cups and memorial trophies. There were smaller artifacts, too, in all of Frank Margineaux's clubs. Small silver bowls from the club races, from the junior division — small bowls to encourage the pursuit of trophies in young people, gestures of affection from trophy-rich fathers to sons with new muscles and the old itch of aspiration. So many artifacts! And so many names! The names were all there on the bowls and the urns: Dolphin, Ponor, Framod, Pale, alone and in combination. At the top of the list, the great names, separate and distinct: Karl G. Ponor, Severus Dolphin, Peter D. Framod, Anthony D. Pale, the richest names of the city — not the oldest, but the richest. Farther down, they combined: Ponor Pale Dolphin, Framod Dolphin, Severus D. Pale. The names were not found equally at all the clubs, of course. The clubs had their distinctions. The clubs narrowed, like a vase. The Seven Nations and the Erie and the Griffin and the Hormin were clubs where there was acceptance but no power: there was no power in a gesture made at the Seven Nations or the Erie or the Griffin or the Hormin. A graceful way of bringing the oar into the catch or the graceful turn of a shoe on a floor had no force at these clubs and disappeared as soon as it was made. This was not true at the Pine Reeves Club and the Turtle Oars and the Augustinian. There were stories about gestures made at the Pine Reeves and the Turtle Oars and the Augustinian. These were stories about grace achieved, and they were pleasant stories, but they were built on an expectant quality. Members of the Pine Reeves and the Turtle Oars and the Augustinian watched themselves, and they watched each other, looking for grace. This was not true at the Lake and the Nile. Within the frame of these two clubs, grace was assumed; and stories (when it was necessary to tell a story) and gestures (when gesture could be demarked from the simple grace of going from one thing to another) had to do not with achievement but with lapses — with the pleasure of affected vulgarity and unexpected choice. The Lake and the Nile shared an eminence of no worry. They had small houses of polished wood and memberships of Dolphins and Ponors and Framods and Pales (no Rapics or Jandons belonged, but some unknown people were elected because they were pretty), and their members spoke to each other in a special language that was like baby talk, in which the clubs themselves were called "Lakers" and "Nilers," while members were called "Lakes" and "Niles." The Lake and the Nile had a prestige and a power of myth unequalled in the history of the city. The Lake and the Nile were in existence for ninety-three years from the day of their founding until they were purchased, along with the lesser clubs, by Frank Margineaux.

That night's boat-club party was held at the Pine Reeves Club, which was in one of the most secure buildings controlled by the Margineaux brothers, and it was not a success. Mr. Frank Margineaux was there early — that could have been the start of the problem. He was drunk and his shoes were covered with mud and his shirt was out, and when his girlfriend called his attention to this he ripped his shirt off as though it were deadly to him. Some girls came and did a circus act, but everyone had seen it before and the animals looked bored. Then a group of people got stuck in an elevator and there wasn't anything to be done about it, so everyone had to listen to people banging and yelling all night. Suki Framod, who did publicity for Frank Margineaux, pulled circuit breakers until she found one that cut off the alarm bell so at least that couldn't go on ringing, but some of the special effects were on the same circuit, so she had to turn it back on.

"Things are really tacky a lot of times," a muscular boy in a satin rowing outfit said to Suki.

"Really," said Suki.

When Mr. Sal Margineaux arrived, Mr. Frank Margineaux had gone to stand in a corner. His shirt was off and he wouldn't put it back on, and he was holding a little silver bowl, holding it like a baby, and crying and crying. Suki took Sal Margineaux over to him. She looked at Frank. "He's just completely lost it," she said.

"Is that right?" Sal Margineaux asked quietly. "Have you completely lost it, Frank?"

Frank Margineaux nodded his head and hugged the bowl tighter and cried some more.

"We've tried a lot of things," Suki said. "We had a circus and then we had some new special effects and then we had some of the oar boys involved with the special effects. And I gave him a present. I had this bowl at home that belonged to my grandfather or something, and I had his name put on it, and the date. And I gave it to him. That's what he's holding, I think." Suki paused. "I've really made an effort," she said.

"I think he's been under a lot of stress," the boy in the satin rowing costume said.

"Which is too bad, because I really dig Frank," Suki said.

Sal Margineaux went and sat at a polished wood table.

He picked the table because there was only one chair at it. He stayed there a long time. "Margineaux Corporation Was Going Great Guns," he said finally.

Things went downhill at the party. It was discovered that the elevator that was stalled was the only elevator big enough to take down the animals that had been involved in the circus, so the animals just roamed around. And then there was a rumor that the people in the elevator had a really heavy scene going, and people tried to get into the elevator, and when that didn't work someone tried to get the people inside the elevator to describe what they were doing in a graphic way, but then it turned out that they weren't having a scene in the elevator after all and that it was just a matter of claustrophobia and panic in the elevator and didn't have anything to do with getting it on, so people got depressed and wandered off and the party went downhill.

Suki Framod tried to cheer up Frank Margineaux by reading him the press release she had typed up for the party, but he just kept crying and crying and she had to give up. "It was one of the most unusual and vivid parties of the Little Season," she read. "Really on the edge." But he just kept crying and crying and she had to give up.

Mr. Sal Margineaux left the party. He left the building. He walked down the stairs — that could have been the beginning of the problem. He felt something rising in him, something like caution. He put one foot ahead of the other. At each step there was a little clink, one result of the brass decoration on his polished shoes. Sometimes the clink was a comfort, but sometimes it echoed on the steps and was alarming. After a time, there was a scream from where the elevator was stuck. Everything was silent for a moment then, because the scream had been very loud and not like a scream rising naturally from a heavy scene but more like a scream rising from panic and disappointed caution. Sal Margineaux felt something rising in him, and after a moment he was able to understand that it was caution. That could have been the beginning of the problem.

He went for a walk — that could have been the beginning of the problem. He walked to a part of the city that was owned by Margineaux Corporation but was not yet secure. The required construction, the required matting, the required rhythms of upheaval and fencing had not been arranged for. In some places there was fencing, but it stopped short. In some places there was matting, but it stopped short. In some places the streets had been taken up, but little patches of street broke through in places, like an orderly rash. Buildings remained. Signs remained. There was a smell, too — an old smell. It was the smell of the Framod Packing Corporation, the ancient slaughterhouse, a giant presence in the industry, one of the three largest provisioners to the Army during the Second World War but then a victim of huge insecure premises and bad marketing decisions.

Sal Margineaux walked on a patch of street, avoiding the cracks, jumping over the cracks, smiling slightly as he landed on a safe place. "Great guns," he said to himself. "Great guns, great guns, great guns, great guns, great guns, great guns," he said to himself. He used something like a singsong voice as he went along, avoiding the cracks. "Great guns, great guns, great guns," he said. He tried to think of a rhyme for "guns" so he could make up a little song, but he had to give that up. He stopped. He looked up and saw the lights on in Van Rayn Street. It comforted him to think that theatres could be open so late, and he decided that he would go to a movie.

He had to walk a long way. At first, he walked directly toward the theatre with the most lights, which was the Luxor-Karnak, but when he came up to Van Rayn Street he saw that the fencing and the matting were in place all along Van Rayn Street and that to get to the theatre he would have to try to climb the fence, which was a fence built not to be climbed, or he would have to walk to a place where the fencing stopped short. He walked for a long while along the fence without finding the end of it. He could see Van Rayn Street, but the theatres were behind him. As he walked, he could see Van Rayn Street get more and more inconsequential until it was almost nothing. There were boardinghouses, and then there were fewer boardinghouses and more gaps; there were taverns with lighted signs — signs with little cocktail glasses, or little poodles, or little clefs and notes —

and then the bars had unlighted signs and were marked as bars only by open doors and music coming out and men standing in front. Then the street signs changed, and instead of saying "Van Rayn Street," they said "Armed Memorial Boulevard." Sal Margineaux looked at one of these signs for a long time, because he was a man who studied street maps and the name was unknown to him. Soon after the signs changed to "Armed Memorial Boulevard," the fence stopped short, and Sal Margineaux crossed to the street and walked back toward the Luxor-Karnak.

The Luxor-Karnak was like a palace. The lobby was that big. There was a huge entrance hall, which led to another hall, which looked up two stories — but that was just part of it. There were two sets of stairs, which led to the balcony — but that was just part of it. Everything was in gold and there were gold statues of the Pharaoh Ramses — but that was just part of it. There was a special room for a display of jewels of the world, and the men's lounge had a smoking room with a decorative theme that made use of gold statues of the god Horus. The women's lounge was dedicated to Nefertiti. And that was just part of it. Everything was kept up well at the Luxor-Karnak. Ushers wore stiff white shirtfronts and stiff standing collars and maroon captain's jackets with "Luxor-Karnak" in gold script. The balcony was closed, though, and the special room for the display of jewels of the world was closed. People sat in the orchestra or stood in the back of the orchestra. Sal

Margineaux went in and sat toward the front, at first, where there weren't many people. On the screen a woman with hair piled on top of her head was welcoming a girl to a party.

WOMAN: I'm so glad you could join our little group. Robert has told us so much about you.
GIRL: Nothing bad, I hope!
WOMAN: Here, let me take your things.

Then the girl took a drink from a waiter and talked to a man called Dr. Helmsy and a man called Sven and a woman called Frieda.

FRIEDA: Is this your first time here?
GIRL: Yes.
FRIEDA: Robert has such good taste.
GIRL: You flatter me!
FRIEDA: Here, let me freshen your drink.

Watching this, Sal Margineaux began to shake and then to cry. He got up to leave, but it was hard to leave, because the back of the orchestra was very crowded. A crowd of old men stood there, making a kind of pattern. They coughed sometimes and talked quietly to themselves. They mentioned the names of streets. "I used to stand at Frangen and Upland Hover," one man said. "That was a nice corner."

"I stood at Arthur and Pulh."

"I stood at Arthur and Gorhn."

"Arthur and Josylyn."

"Arthur and Kenmur."

"Turly."

"James."

They mentioned other names. Parkway, Lones, Sury, Gorman, and Herts were some of the names they mentioned.

On the screen, the girl was surprised to see her escort tied up on a table.

> GIRL: Is that Robert?
> SVEN: Incredible, isn't it.
> FRIEDA: Here, let me help you off with that.

The old men looked at the movie as though it was what they expected to see, and then they looked away from the movie. The movie went off after a while, and the men didn't change their stance. Then another movie went on. Sal Margineaux went through the crowd of old men, and they just gave way and he went right through. Sal Margineaux could hear them naming the streets that had heaved up, though, and that made him uneasy. He could see them forming a grid of corners, and that made him uneasy. "Great guns," he said. One old man looked up when he said that — looked right at Mr. Sal Margineaux, right at him — and then walked up to Mr.

Margineaux, who didn't do a thing. "Margineaux Corporation Was Going Great Guns. Then It Suddenly Ran Aground," Sal Margineaux said.

The next day, against the advice of his bankers, Mr. Sal Margineaux began to assemble papers designed to effect the acquisition by Margineaux Corporation of the vast, aged Shield Fresh Company, where pigs had been slaughtered for a hundred years, where cattle had been slaughtered for a hundred years, where generations of men had slaughtered pigs and ripped open their stomachs and sent their entrails down chute after chute to cellars, where use was made of them, where use was made of everything.

Two days after this, in the afternoon, Sal Margineaux arrived on West Cottage Avenue. He came on foot. He walked carefully and tried to avoid the mud. In some places the grade had been maintained and there was no problem; in other places the grade had sunk but there was a wall broad enough to walk on and there was no problem. At times, however, the grade sank beneath him, and at times there was no passage except through mud, and then there was a problem. Because Sal Margineaux did not perfectly understand the numbering system in use on West Cottage Avenue, he was surprised to find that he had a long walk and not a short one; because he did not understand that West Cottage Avenue was aristocratic only between Sixteenth Street and Twenty-second Street, he was surprised to find that for much of his way he passed only small sunken bungalows — picked over, empty, and sunk, in some examples, up to the lintel of the doorway. This made him furious. It made him furious to feel the weight of the mud on his shoes. It made him furious that the brass on his shoes made no noise, no reassuring clink — that the brass was gagged in mud. When he came to the house he wanted, he hated that, too — hated the brick and the limestone and the intricate railing on the roof and the curved glass bowing out in what must have been a conservatory. He stood outside the house and did not move for a long while. He stood still and waited for the danger to subside. The danger was that his mind was not on his business. The danger was that the contradiction of hating poverty and wealth at the same time would unfocus his special way of using energy quickly for one purpose. He stood silently until he could feel the various hatreds begin to subside. After a while, he began not to recognize the brick or the limestone. The annoyance of the cast-iron decoration and the curved windows of the conservatory fell from his memory. That made the danger less. But for his sense of the mud to weaken took much longer, and it did not completely leave him for all the time he stood quietly and played with words in his mind, for all the time he spent taking words and phrases, long words with a long story, proper names some of them, and reducing them in his mind to quick contractions with no meaning except what he chose to assign. He stood at the door for more than three hours. During this time, he was observed from a window of amber glass by an old woman, who went to the door when he rang the bell at last.

He had papers, of course. Shown to a room where the light was blue, where the sun was filtered through vast windows of stained glass of a rich, deep blue, he had to hold himself quiet again to adjust, but then he took the brown leather envelope from under his arm and took several packets of papers from it. It was then that he noticed that there was nowhere to put them down. He had at his disposal many gestures to use in placing papers on a table or a desk. But there were no tables or desks in this room, and no chairs. It was utterly bare and utterly clean. The walls were covered with a rich blue damask, which looked quite new and fresh; the walls were framed by finely carved pilasters of dark wood, which seemed newly polished; the ceiling was of the same dark wood — dark polished beams running the long distance from front to back like expensive railroad tracks. And the glory of the floor! He noticed the glory of the floor, which was an intricate parquet — a floor like a rug of silk wood, a floor like a woven floor, woven to an incredible closeness, enclosed at the walls by a small strip of deep red marble.

Unsure, Sal Margineaux put the papers on the floor. This was perhaps the beginning of the problem. He noticed that the papers looked weak on the floor. This was perhaps the beginning of the problem. He noticed, also, the mud on his pant legs and on his shoes. He saw that some of the mud had dried and had flaked off on the floor around his foot and that some of the mud was still wet. He saw that the old woman, who was Bethe Ponor, last granddaughter of Karl Goethe Ponor, who had come from New England and who had seen the need for a man who could slaughter cattle, and who had started that business, the Shield Fresh Company — the ancient slaughterhouse, a giant presence in the industry, the largest provisioner to the Army for years and years, but more and more a victim of huge insecure premises and bad marketing decisions — he saw that the old woman had put the power of his papers out of her mind and was looking closely at the mud.

"Some of our visitors are not used to our mud," she said.

Sal Margineaux left the house, leaving the papers. The trip away from the house was difficult. Night began to fall, and it turned out that the sunken bungalows gave shelter to dangerous squatters after dark. From the bungalows came scraps of song, which made Sal Margineaux furious and unsure. That may have been the beginning of the problem. "It hurts me, too" was one scrap of song he heard. "When I was quite young" was another. "Can't go down, can't go down, by myself" was another. There was one patch where many men were talking. Sal Margineaux, disliking this direction, turned around and walked back the other way. That may have been the beginning of the problem. As he turned, he noticed the figure of an old woman moving quickly across the avenue, up a set of stairs that led to no house — only a set of limestone stairs, narrowing gently in a curve toward the top step, where the fragment of a porch and three short columns together rose above the balustrade. Sal Margineaux watched the figure of the woman without controlling his thoughts — that may have been the beginning of the problem. He watched the woman bend down and leave something on the fragment of porch. He watched her move quickly down the steps to the street and then quickly to a spot next door, where there was nothing. He watched the woman bend down quickly, and he watched her as she moved quickly away down the street, stopping at measured distances to bend down again. He went toward the limestone steps where he had seen her first. That may have been the beginning of the problem. He crossed the avenue without watching where he stepped, and he found himself deep in mud. Then he tried to step where he remembered that the figure of the woman had stepped, and he found himself in mud as deep as before. When he reached the limestone steps, he was furious, and for the first time in many years he was furious at himself, which may have been the beginning of the problem. At the top of the stairs, he looked down the avenue, and it seemed to him that the woman was looking at him from the half-darkness, although he could not see her. He looked around on the fragment of porch. The porch was covered with small pieces of pasteboard: hundreds of pieces of pasteboard, maybe more than that. Some were fresh and still had their edge and their snap; others had begun to decompose. Each one was the same; each one bore the name "Miss Ponor" in neat gothic lettering, and each one had been folded at the left corner to show that it had been delivered in person. Sal Margineaux kicked at the layers of cards with his foot, but they seemed to go deep, layer upon layer, like an ancient compost pile, and he gave up. Then he ran down the avenue, and after a time he saw the figure of the woman. He walked behind her. She seemed to know places in the street that would exactly support her weight; certainly she did not sink into the mud. She seemed to be singing the scrap of a song. When he came closer, he heard that she was singing in a deep voice — almost the voice of a man, almost the voice of a Negro man. "When things go wrong, go wrong with you, it hurts me, too," she sang. Sal Margineaux was made furious by the song and came very close to the old woman. "I hope you liked the papers," he said.

"Oh, I understand papers," the old woman said without turning her head. She walked at a simple pace, but because he was so tired and so defeated by the mud, it seemed to him that she moved away at an astonishing speed. After a moment, she turned and said in a high, clear voice, "I would naturally help you to your destination, but I do not ever go beyond Sixteenth Street." Then she went into her house.

She went up to the top of the house, where she sat

for the night with her father, the son of the founder. Her father had brought stained glass to the city, had made stained glass the vogue. He was assumed to be dead but he was not dead. He was not known because he never once went to the stockyards from the time of inheriting his vast fortune, but lay day after day, year after year, in a room of incomparable beauty — quite beautiful himself in a curious wrapping of white cambric. She went to her father. Her father was her friend. She told him stories through the night. At dawn, she left him, but for a long while during the morning the momentum of the night's storytelling stayed with her, so that she spoke constantly to herself, out loud. At about eleven o'clock, she said, "I understand bullies. I have a friend who is a bully. Not a bully — *like* a bully. Like a bully with a pure heart." Then she was silent for the rest of the day.